More praise for *Gh...*

'A masterful piece ...
as one of our best ...

'It's writing that, ...
world and acute ale... ...
recalls the early ficti... ...rings enriching
complexity to this ... ...ing menace' *Sunday Times*

'A spellbinding tale awaits within' 'Book of the Year', *Herald*

'Moss's brevity is admirable, her language pristine. This story
lingers, leaving its own ghosts, but with important lessons for
the future of idealising the past' Sinéad Gleeson, *Irish Times*

'Sublime ... *Ghost Wall* packs an incredible emotional punch'
Big Issue

'Brief and entirely compelling ... [An] intensely charged and
menacing little book' *Metro*

'Devastating' *Spectator*

'Slim, unnerving ... an intense and menacing book – the
sort that's best read in one sitting' *Tatler*

'Subtly chilling ... By entangling us so closely with Sylvie's
individual plight, Moss leads us deftly towards more radical
insights; in hoping for Silvie's liberation, we are also fighting
back against insidious narratives that seem all too powerful
in our own world today' *TLS*

Ghost Wall

Sarah Moss

GRANTA

Granta Publications, 12 Addison Avenue, London, W11 4QR

First published in Great Britain by Granta Books, 2018
This paperback published by Granta Books, 2019

A CIP catalogue record for this book
is available from the British Library

9 8 7 6 5 4 3 2 1

ISBN 978 1 78378 446 2
eISBN 978 1 78378 447 9

Printed

THEY BRING HER out. Not blindfolded, but eyes widened to the last sky, the last light. The last cold bites her fingers and her face, the stones – not the last stones – bruise her bare feet. She stumbles. They hold her up. No need to be rough, everyone knows what is coming. From deep inside her body, from the cord in her spine and the wide blood-ways under the ribs, from the emptiness of her womb and the rising of her chest, she shakes. A body in fear. They lead the fearful body over the turf and along the track, her bare feet numb to most of the pain of rock and sharp rushes. Chanting rises, the drums sound slow, unsyncopated with the last panic of her heart. Others follow, wrapped against the cold, dark figures processing into the dusk.

On arrival, they strip her. It is easy; they have put her into a loose tunic. Her body is white in the pale red light,

1

solid against the wisps of fog and the tracery of reed. She tries to cover herself with her hands, and is not allowed. One holds her while the other binds her. Her breathing is accelerating, its condensation settling on her face. All of them are accompanied by their exhalations, slowly dissolving into the air. They turn her to face the crowd, they display her to her neighbours and her family, to the people who held her hands as she learnt to walk, taught her to dip her bread in the pot and wipe her lips, to weave a basket and gut a fish. She has played with the children who now peep at her from behind their mothers, has murmured prayers for them as they were being born. She has been one of them, ordinary. Her brother and sisters watch her flinch as the men take the blade, lift the pale hair on the left side of her head and cut it away. They scrape the skin bare. She doesn't look like one of them now. She shakes. They tuck the hair into the rope around her wrists.

She is whimpering, keening. The sound echoes across the marsh, sings through the bare branches of rowan and birch.

There are no surprises.

They place another rope around her neck, hold the knife up to the setting sun as it edges behind the rocks.

What is necessary is on hand, the sharpened willow withies, the pile of stones, the small blades and the large. The stick for twisting the rope.

Not yet. There is an art to holding her in the place she is entering now, on the edge of the water-earth, in the time and space between life and death, too late to return to the living and not time, not yet, not for a while, to be quite dead.

DARKNESS WAS A long time coming. The fire crackled, transparent against the trees, its purpose no more, no less, than ceremonial. We had been pushed away from each other by the heat that no-one wanted. Woodsmoke stung my eyes and the rock dug into my backside, the rough tunic itchy under my thighs. I slipped my foot out of its moccasin and pointed my toes towards the fire for no reason, to see how it felt. You can't be cold, my father said, though it was he who had lit the fire and insisted that we gather around it. I can, I thought, if I've a mind, but I said no, Dad, I'm not cold. Through the flames, I could see the boys, talking to each other and drawn back almost into the trees as if they were thinking of melting into the woods and creeping off somewhere to do some boys' thing at which I would probably be more skilled. My mother sat on the stone where my father had told her to sit, tunic rucked unbecomingly above her fat white knees, staring into the flames as people do; it was boring and my father was holding us all there, bored, by force of will. Where do you think you're going, he said as I stood up. I need, I said, to pee, and he grunted and glanced towards the boys, as if the very mention of biological functions might incite their adolescent passions. Just make sure you go out of sight, he said.

Within a few days, our feet would wear a path through the trees to the stream, but that first night there was moss under foot, squashy in the dim light, and patches of wild strawberries so ripe and red they were still visible in the dusk, as if glowing. I squatted to gather a handful and wandered on, picking them out of my palm with my lips, kissing my own hand. Bats flashed through the space between branches, mapping depth into the flat sky: I could still hear them then. It was odd to walk in the thin leather shoes, only a layer of borrowed – stolen – skin between my feet and the sticks and stones, the damp patches and soft places of the woods. I came to the stream and squatted beside it, dipped my fingers, listened. Water over rock and peat, leaves stirring behind me and over my head, a sheep calling on the hill. Fresh dew came through my shoes. The stream tugged at my fingertips and the heather explored my legs, bare under the tunic. It was not that I didn't understand why my father loved these places, this outdoor life. It was not that I thought houses were better.

When I returned to the fire, my mother was kneeling at its side, not propitiating the gods but hefting slabs of green turf from a pile. Give us a hand, Sil, she said, he says if you do it right you can cover it for the night and pull the turfs off in the morning, he says that's how they always did it, them. In the old days. Yeah, I said, kneeling beside her, and I dare say he didn't say as how there was someone to show you, in the old days, how they didn't just give out instructions and bugger off. She sat back. Well, she said, but they'd have known, wouldn't they, back then, not have needed telling, you'd have learnt it at your mam's side and don't use language like that, he'll hear you.

We were sleeping in the roundhouse, my parents and I. The students had built it earlier in the year, as part of a course on 'experiental archaeology', but they had been firmly resistant to my father's view that everyone should sleep in it together. There was no reason, my father said, to think that Ancient British households had been

6

organized like modern families, if the students wanted a real experience they should join us on the splintery bunks they had built and padded with deerskins donated by the anachronistic local lord of the manor. Or at least, since the lord of the manor lived in London and certainly didn't spend his summers in Northumberland, donated by some servant on his behalf. Professor Slade said ah well, after all authenticity was impossible and not really the goal anyway, the point was to have a flavour of Iron Age life and perhaps some insight into particular processes or technologies. Let the students sleep in their tents if they prefer, he said, there were almost certainly Iron Age tents also. Skin tents, Dad said, none of this fancy nylon stuff. The tent we used on our holidays was made of canvas the colour of apricots and possibly left over from the Second World War. I had noticed that the students had pitched their inauthentic colourful and waterproof nylon tents in the clearing below our hut, screened by trees and hillside from both the roundhouse and the Professor's larger tent nearer the track where he kept his car. I could sleep in one too, Dad, I said, give you and Mum some privacy, but Dad didn't want privacy, he wanted to be able to see what I was up to. Don't be daft, he said, of course you can't sleep wi' the lads, shame on you. Anyway privacy's a fancy modern idea, exactly what we're getting away from, everyone trying to hide away and do what they want, you'll be joining in with the rest of us. I do not know what my father thought I might want to do in those days but he devoted considerable attention to making sure I couldn't do it.

The bunks were exactly as uncomfortable as you'd expect. I had refused to sleep wearing the scratchy tunic that my father insisted in the absence of any evidence whatsoever to be the Ancient British nightdress as well as daywear, but even through brushed cotton pyjamas the straw-stuffed sack was prickly, smelt like a farmyard and rustled as if there were small mammals frisking in it every time I moved. The darkness in the hut was complete, disconcerting; I lay on my back moving my hands in front of my face and saw nothing at all. My father turned, sighed and began to snore, an irregular bovine noise that made the idea of sleep ridiculous. Mum, I whispered, Mum, you awake? Shh, she hissed back, go to sleep. I can't, I said, he's too loud, can't you give him a shove. Shh, she said, go to sleep Silvie, close your eyes. I turned onto my side, facing the wall, and then back because it didn't feel like a good idea to have my back to the darkness like that. What if there were

8

insects in the straw, ticks or fleas, what if they got inside my pyjamas, what if there was one now, on my foot, maybe all the way up my leg, jumping and biting and jumping, and on my back, coming through the sack, several of them, on my shoulders and my neck – Silvie, hissed Mum, stop wriggling like that and go to sleep, you're getting on my nerves summat proper. He's getting on my nerves summat proper, I said, they can probably hear him in Morbury, I don't know how you put up with it. There was a grunt, a shift. The snoring stopped and we both lay still, frozen. Pause. Maybe he's not going to breathe again, I thought, maybe that's it, the end, but then it started again, a serrated knife through cardboard.

When I woke up there was light seeping around the sheepskin hanging over the door. They probably didn't actually have sheep, the Professor had said, but since we weren't allowed to kill animals using Iron Age technologies we would have to take what we could get and sheepskins are a lot easier to pick up on the open market than deerskins. While I was glad we weren't going to be hacking the guts out of deer in the woods with flint blades, I thought the Professor's dodging of bloodshed pretty thoroughly messed up the idea that our experiences that summer were going to rediscover the lifeways of pre-modern hunter gatherers. The clue, I muttered, is in the name, you know, *hunter* gatherers? What was that, Silvie, said Dad, would you like to repeat what you just said to Professor Slade? Oh, please, call me Jim, said Professor Slade, and don't worry, I have teenagers myself, I know what it's like. Yeah, I'd thought, but your teenagers aren't here, are they, gone off somewhere nice with their mum I don't doubt, France or Italy probably. I turned onto my back, which was stiff, and bashed my elbow on the wooden ledge holding the straw sack. I wriggled cautiously over the splinters and stood barefoot on the bare earth, dry and dusty. There was barely enough light to see Mum's and Dad's bunks empty, the outline of the central pole disappearing into the darkness under the roof. Some of the Iron Age people kept their ancestors' half-smoked corpses up in the rafters, bound in a squatting position, peering down empty-eyed. Some of the houses had bits of dead children buried under the doorway, for luck, or for protection from something worse.

Mum was crouching at the side of the fire, blowing on the embers, a pile of turfs at her side. So it does work, I said, how did you get the turfs off without burning yourself? She took another breath, leant forward and blew through pursed lips to the fire's glowing base. The embers brightened in the sunlight. Leaf-shadows flickered. With great difficulty, she said, here, you try, it's knackering my knees like nobody's business. I went down onto my knees and elbows, hoped none of the students would come up and see my backside stuck up in the air, blew, and again. Watch your hair, said Mum. I took another breath, smelling earth and green wood. There, I said. Flames. What's for breakfast? She shook her head. Porridge, she said, well I suppose you'd call it gruel, there's no milk and it's not oats, more like rye I think or let's hope not barley else it'll not be cooked this side of Christmas. Any honey, I asked; I would generally eat porridge only if it came with an equal volume of golden syrup, though Dad not so much liked it plain and heavily salted as believed in it the way other people believe in homeopathy or holy water. All this cancer, he said of Mum's newly diagnosed friend, folk need roughage, weren't never meant for all that processed muck, breakfast cereals and what have you, I'd as soon eat the box. Mum, what about dinner, I said, and tea? It'll be whatever you gather this morning, she said, maybe fish, there must be berries, this time of year. You don't, I thought, *gather* fish, there has to be murder done

11

and you won't be the one doing it, Mum, but instead of saying so I put a couple more kindling sticks on the fire and one of the nice dry logs the students had chopped as part of their archaeological experience.

Mum started pushing at the big stones at the edge of the fireplace and I went to help. They need to be in far enough to balance the pot, she said, he says we'll be making a frame to hang it from later. Or a whatsit, a trivet. Out of what, I said, he's never planning on blacksmithing, is he? Smithing was one of his fascinations. He remembered, he said, the last blacksmith in the village, who gave up a few years after the war, remembered being allowed to stand in the doorway watching the metal turn from solid to glowing liquid and back, the hiss and sudden billow of steam, the man's scarred hands. It were sacred work, he said, in the old days, fire and liquid and tempered blades. Mum shrugged. He said to use stones for now. Bring us the pot, Silvie, it's right by the door. The pot was iron, very heavy. I squatted, embraced it warmly, lifted with my knees but of course the thing was still ridiculous. Bloody hell, Mum, I said, how about a bit of toast instead, shove some sausages on sticks, but I could see from her face that I shouldn't have opened my mouth. Dad was behind me. You know fine well they didn't have toast, he said, and if I catch you sneaking off to eat rubbish there'll be trouble, is that clear? Yes Dad, I said, sorry, only joking. Well don't, he said, it's not funny. And go dress yourself, put your tunic on, I don't want to see those pyjamas and I certainly don't want the Professor seeing them. The Professor, I could have pointed out, was the one wearing tennis socks because he thought the moccasins might give him blisters if he didn't, but I went into the hut, rummaged in the suitcase Gran had passed on to Mum and put on knickers and a bra before the scratchy tunic. There'd been a discussion about that in the kitchen at home, weeks back. But you'll be wanting us in our own undies, Mum had said to Dad, anyone might see anything else, those lads and our Silvie. She'd won a concession for toothbrushes too: stands to reason they didn't worry themselves with that, weren't going to live long enough to lose their teeth anyroad. And also, eventually, tampons, once Dad had pointed out once again that in the old days women weren't going round forever bleeding all over the place anyway, all those doings starting later when there was less to eat and everyone better for it, and then women in the family way and feeding babies the way nature intended as long as they could, which was also what he said whenever he caught me or mum buying sanitary protection. Women managed well enough, he said, back in the day, without spending money on all that, ends up on the beaches in the end, right mucky. Or they died, I said, in childbirth, what with the rickets and no caesarians, but you won't be wanting me pregnant, Dad, for authenticity's sake? He'd put down the list he was writing, set the pen parallel to it on the counter and stood up, formal. Hush, said Mum, cheek, but she was too late, the slap already airborne. You court it, she'd say, you go just one step too far, what do you expect?

Whether the gruel was rye or barley, it was still resisting the actions of heat and water when the students turned up. Grains bobbled like dead maggots. Did we put too much water in, I asked Mum, isn't it meant to be going kind of gluey? You'll have to be up and about earlier than this tomorrow, you two, Dad said, folk need to eat, this won't do. I could see he wanted us to do something, speed up the heating of water and the expansion of grain. The agitation of molecules, I thought, remembering Chemistry GCSE. I took the carved paddle and stirred, made the maggots swim in one direction. It wasn't fair for Dad to tell us off for oversleeping when he'd made us leave our watches at home and kept talking about the benefits of life without clocks. Folk lived by their bellies and the sun, then, weren't forever counting off the minutes, folk knew patience in the old days.

We heard voices, laughter – I glanced at Dad, who didn't always like it when people laughed – and the students came up the path. Pete, I remembered, Dan, and the girl was Molly. Last night, the first night, they had been in jeans but today they were wearing their tunics and looking no less silly than I did. Gorgeous legs, said Dan to Pete as they came out of the trees. Yeah well, Pete said, you're flashing us your tits mate, think you've got something a bit wrong there. Tits. I looked again at Dad but he wasn't looking, wasn't listening. Molly came behind them, tunic pinned with a CND badge and her fair hair in two plaits secured with elastic bobbles with red plastic cherries on them. There were colours in her hair like the grain in polished pine and you could follow them all the way down the plaits. I'm sorry, said Mum, I'm late with breakfast, it'll be a while yet. No, said Dan, it's fine, we don't have meal times, Jim keeps saying. We just eat when it's ready. Jim, I thought, Professor Slade. Can I help you, Alison, said Molly, really, there's no reason you should do it all. Mum's eyes met mine. Alison. My friends called her Mrs Hampton. No, she said, you're all right, happen I can stir a pan, you get on. They sat in the sun, the students, chatted, teased each other, used some words I'd only read, laughed when they felt like it. I pottered, gathering kindling, more or less, staying far enough away not to look as if I wanted to join in but mostly near enough to hear what they were saying. Plans for later in the summer, 'going travelling' as if just moving around counted as a rational use of time and money. Inter-rail passes, Rome and Paris. Now you can go to Prague and Budapest too, said Dan, my sister did last year, before everyone started going. Pete had already been to Berlin, after his exams, had seen some of the wall come down. I've got a chunk of it, he said, at home, it's pink because there were murals and graffiti on it already, it was dead cool, we sat on it and there were people with guitars and singing, beers all night, they don't have closing time there. Only it's actually a bit sad because everyone's just nicking bits of it now, the wall, and if they keep going there'll be even less of it left than Hadrian's by the end of the century, you could kind of see the streets joining up again, fusing. I want to go there, said Molly, I'd like to see it for myself. Going to Berlin, I thought. How do you get to Berlin, can you start at the bus stop, do you take an aeroplane or the train, several trains? I knew many of the British isles, Holy Island and Anglesey, the Orkneys and several of the Hebrides, but I had never been overseas. We didn't have passports. Where was the money coming from, what did Dan and Pete and Molly's parents think of these plans? Dad went off into the woods, stiff-necked, and Mum's face darkened, her shoulders hunched as she stirred the pot, as if there were clouds gathering that only she could see.

The Professor appeared after breakfast and started organising people in a way that made me wonder if he thought there were Iron Age professors, or maybe as if he couldn't imagine that there were circumstances in which qualities other than being posh and having read a lot might put a person in charge of everyone else. My dad, I thought, knew as much as anyone about living wild off the land, foraging and fishing and finding your way. You and you, go look for edible plants in this area, said the Prof. Make sure you're back by half-three, the basket-weaver's coming to do a workshop. Bill, come with me for fishing. Alison – he looked perplexed, perhaps suddenly unsure if he was allowed to tell Dad's wife what to do – could you maybe, well, sort out the camp a bit, if you don't mind? What about me, I said, what will I do? Go with the foraging party, said Dad, maybe you'll learn summat, but you're not to wander off and don't make a nuisance of yourself, this might be fun and games to you but it's these folks' work, their studies, I'll not have you messing around. It's not a game to me either, I said, we have to eat, course I'll go foraging.

They had the OS map and a forager's handbook. Well, said the Prof, only compensating for the local knowledge Ancient British youth would have had, your education isn't going to help you much with what they'd have known since childhood. We each took a skin bag and set out along the footpath towards the moor. There were, of course, dry stone walls and fields of cattle and a line of pylons against the sky and indeed a tarmac road on which one red car crawled near the horizon. If the occupants saw us, I thought, first they'd think we were ghosts and then they might wonder if they'd driven back in time. My hands and teeth clenched with the strength of my hope that they would not see us. The day was already hot, sweat prickling on my back and heather floating in mirage above the nearest rise. Underfoot, the path was soft with dust, white roots jutting like birdbones from the dry earth.

So, said Dan, Silvie, what, short for Sylvia? Sulevia, I said. I was about to say, as I had been doing since I first started school, she was an Ancient British goddess, my dad chose it, but they were already exchanging glances. Sulevia's a local deity, said Dan, Jim was talking about her the other day. Northumbrian goddess of springs and pools, co-opted by the Romans, said Molly. So you come from round here? No, I said, we're to the west, Burnley way? She shook her head. You've heard of Rochdale then, I said, but she hadn't. Near Manchester then, I said, northwards. Yeah, she said, OK but your dad's not a historian, right, how did he know about her if you're not local? I could feel myself turning red. He's a bus driver, I said, history's just a hobby, he wanted me to have a proper native British name. I saw glances again. What, I said, people have all sorts of weird names, at least it's not some random word, River or Rainbow or that. Yeah, said Dan, it's just interesting, I've never met anyone with that kind of name.

Well, I said, you have now. And look, there's a hawk, I think it's a sparrowhawk, look at the wings. I squinted into the sun and pointed, tracked its ascent into the darkness at the top of the sky.

Good eyes, said Pete. Right, a *proper British* name. What's he mean by that, then? Nothing, I said, he likes British prehistory, he thought it was a shame the old names had gone. Right, said Pete, you mean he likes the idea that there's some original Britishness somewhere, that if he goes back far enough he'll find someone who wasn't a foreigner. You know it's not really British, right? I mean, Sulevia, it's obviously just a version of Sylvia which means – *of the woods* in Latin, I said, yes, I do know, a Roman corruption of a lost British word. There are actually people who know Latin where I come from, we do have books. I could hear my accent shifting as I spoke to them, talking posh and then getting angry and speaking normally again. My face was going red. Peter, I thought, you know that's really a biblical name, how does it feel to be called a rock, are your parents really into Christianity then?

A raven called and I squinted into the sun. Right above us, there, the sun glinting white on its black wings. It called again, warning or advice: I'd bugger off now if I was you, mate. So it's actually more of a Roman name, Dan said, does he know that? I wriggled my shoulders, as if I could shrug away the questions. Yeah, I said, probably, he does actually know quite a lot about Roman Britain. Why, asked Molly, if he's a bus driver? The pine trees on the ridge bowed and you could see a breath of wind passing over the heather, dying before it reached us. He's interested, of course, I said, that's why we're here. OK, said Pete, fair enough, and we walked in silence for a few minutes. The sun shone. The raven circled low. I ran my hand over my hair to feel the heat it had absorbed. You couldn't really hear our feet on the path, just the movement of skin and cloth, the sound of your own hair against your ears, a grouse startling at our approach. The raven said something derisive and left us to it.

You planning to do archaeology at university then, asked Dan. I shrugged. Dunno, I said, not really planning to go, I don't think, I'd rather just get a job, get started. There were still grants then, it would have been a way of escaping Dad's control, but also, it seemed to me, a way of postponing what I imagined as real life, extending the adolescence I couldn't wait to leave. I probably won't get the grades anyway, I said. Stop questioning me, I thought, but I didn't quite know how to ask anything of my own. How do you leave home, how do you get away, how do you not go back? What's the best way to Berlin from here? Where are we actually going, I asked, what are we actually looking for? Actually, I thought, stop saying actually, it's stupid. You heard the man, said Dan, edible plants, and he kept

21

going as if he knew what he was doing and the rest of us kept following him.

The sun strengthened as we reached mid-morning, bathing moor and trees and fields in summer yellow. There was no shade, I remember everything a little flattened as if in one of those over-exposed photos it used to be possible to take. There won't be any berries or anything on the moor, will there, it's just heather and peat, isn't it, no point going up there, said Pete, and I waited and glanced around at the others before I said well, you've probably thought about this and I dare say I'm wrong, but would it be worth looking for bilberries, I mean it's probably the wrong time of year, a bit early, specially up here.

Mid-July. The moors above our town were covered with them by early August. Dad didn't like to stop on his walks, hadn't come up here to footle about like an old woman at the market, but he'd slow down while I picked a handful and caught him up, and when we camped in Scotland he'd leave Mum and me half a morning to gather what we could while he went in search of food more exciting to catch.

Oh, you mean blueberries, said Dan, yeah, sure, it's worth a look, where do they grow? I glanced around again. I didn't mean blueberries. I'd never eaten blueberries, which as far as I knew were a kind of American oversized bilberry robust enough for the pies people ate in films. Everyone kept walking. Molly had lifted her face to the sun and half-closed her eyes. No, bilberries, I said, south-facing slopes, usually, sheep like them too, best not to eat them unwashed, there's a parasite in sheep pee. Wow, said Pete, you do know a lot, where'd you learn all this? Dad, I said, my dad taught me.

We followed the green-signposted Public Footpath along a stone wall and over a stile towards the moor. As the hill rose, we could see Roman Dere Street, the road to Hadrian's Wall drawn across the next rise as if it was made of something different from the rest of the landscape, as if someone had drawn it with a ruler on a photo. Dad and I had walked the Wall's whole length, Newcastle to Carlisle, at Easter the previous year. I remembered the approach of this road near the best bit, the section where the steep ground and sudden drops made a millennium's worth of northern farmers not bother themselves to pull down milecastles and miles of dressed stone to build sheep-pens and byres. We had stopped there to eat our sandwiches and I'd half closed my eyes, imagined hearing on the wind the Arabic conversations of the Syrian soldiers who'd dug the ditches and hoisted the stones two thousand years ago. I'd tried to hold the view in my mind and strip the landscape of pylons and church towers, to see through the eyes of the patrolling legion fresh from the Black Forest. They weren't even really Roman, Dad had said, they were from all over the show, North Africa and Eastern Europe and Germany, probably a lot of them didn't even speak proper Latin. There were even Negroes, imagine what the Britons made of that, they'd never have seen the like. We were only two days out from Newcastle, a city that had upset Dad, and I knew better than to challenge him; even the word 'Negro' was already some concession to my ideas because he preferred to use a more offensive term and wait, chin raised, for a reaction. The day we arrived he'd taken me not to the Roman cases in the city museum or to the sorry remnants of the Roman castle under the Victorian railway bridge where we would have been out of the weather, but to the docks, idle and strewn with rubbish. Come on, girl, walk, don't you look away from this. It's only water, won't get further nor skin. This is what there was, this is what's left. The wind from the Siberian steppes sliced across the North Sea to whip us with rain. I had on one of Nan's knitted hats, the sort of thing I wouldn't wear if anyone I knew might see me, but still pain started up in my ears as I followed him across the concrete waste. Cranes reared above us like the ceremonial pillars of a lost civilisation, intricate with rust and disintegration. The windflowers and morning glory that are either holding together or pulling apart England's abandoned buildings and roads and railways flattened under the weather. Look at this, he said, look at it. Used to send ships all over the world from here. Look at it now.

There wasn't a campsite in the city so we spent the first night in a bed and breakfast where there were cigarette burns in the curtains and stains on the nylon sheets. The corner shop sold fruits and vegetables I'd never seen before and smelt of jasmine and spices, but Dad wouldn't go in, wouldn't let me try the milky and pink and green sweets oozing syrup on trays in the window of the Indian takeaway, the twisted orange knots and the silver you were apparently meant to eat. Paki muck, he said, you don't want to know what they put in those, here, since it's the first night I'll treat you to a fish and chips, how about that? With that tartare sauce stuff you like. That'll set you up properly.

It was still raining the next morning when Dad made me take the bacon and toast I couldn't eat and hide it in a shiny paper napkin to make my lunch. We set off along streets in some ways deeply familiar, where front doors opened onto the pavement, back gates onto the ginnel and the houses had one rattling sash window upstairs and one down, the architecture of Victorian poverty, but the voices here were different, the words sung to a tune carried over the sea. Dad's mood lifted through the day as we reached the edge of the city and set out through fields, albeit fields broken by A-roads crossing the landscape on pilings with no way for pedestrians, foot-soldiers, to get across. The Wall was only a ditch, that first day, but at least it was a Roman ditch, a physical manifestation of Ancient British resistance still marked on the land, and you could see Dad drawing strength from it.

We had come up onto the moor tops, where the high ground rolls under a big sky. Walking up there, it feels as if you're being offered on an open hand to the weather, though when you look down there are plenty of soft little hiding places, between the marsh grass in the boggy dips and in the heather, vibrating with bees, on the slopes. Molly pulled a packet of fruit pastilles out of her sheepskin bag and offered it around. There's a petrol station on the road to the village, she said, we can always get more, it's not as if Iron Age foragers wouldn't have gone to Spar if they could. Do they have ice-cream, asked Pete. That's a bit crap, Moll, said Dan, they'd also have had hot showers and hiking boots and microwaves if they could, wouldn't they, I mean people do, when they can. Doubt it, said Molly, chewing, not the hiking boots, anyway, would've felt horrible to them.

She was right. You move differently in moccasins, have a different experience of the relationship between feet and land. You go around and not over rocks, feel the texture, the warmth, of different kinds of reed and grass in your muscles and your skin. The edges of the wooden steps over the stile touch your bones, an unseen pebble catches your breath. You can imagine how a person might learn a landscape with her feet. But we hadn't yet crossed any bog and I was pretty sure it would feel different in winter. They used to stuff their moccasins with hay for insulation. You too, Silvie, said Molly, offering her packet with a red one at the top, have one if you like. Of course I liked.

We found bilberries, growing amongst the heather on a south-facing slope above a stream below some lumps that the map called ROMAN CAMP (rems of). There, I said, the one with the round shiny leaves turning red, the berries are under the leaves, you don't see them at first. Don't be bossy, I told myself, little Miss Know-it-all, but no-one seemed to mind. The leather soles weren't much protection once we'd left the path, and the heather tickled my ankles. I unlaced the shoes, hung them around my neck and picked my way up the stream, teetering on rocky pebbles and cautious over weed. Good idea, said Dan, though given how shallow the stream and strong the sun, the water was remarkably cold. I wondered if they'd done this, the old people, the Ancient Britons, paddled where there was no path, stepped in and out of the water because, as Dad liked to say, your skin's a waterproof membrane, that's what it's there for, to get wet.

Despite what I'd said about the sheep, I ate the berries and so did everyone else. They were warm from the sun, with a bloom on them like skin. Bruised skin. I liked the prickle of the calyx on my tongue, the way they burst in my mouth, the way you don't know until then if it's a bland or a sharp one. Bet you could make good gin with these, said Pete, you know, like with damsons. Did they make alcohol, I asked. Dunno, said Molly, probably, you would, wouldn't you? It's easy enough to do by accident if you're storing fruit and veg. They had rye, I don't know when ergot poisoning started but I'm sure they had some psychotropic stuff. Yeah, I said, actually, my dad says, there were things they gave the bog people before they were sacrificed, to quiet them like, or maybe blunt the pain. Pete held up a bilberry to the sun, squinted at it. Maybe I'll do my thesis on it, he said, that would be fun, do you think you're allowed to do experiential archaeology on drugs if you forage them yourself? Ask Jim, said Molly, he'd like the idea whether you're actually allowed or not, don't you think he probably smokes dope with his friends at home, like after a dinner party, and thinks he's really cool? It'd be pretty good, said Pete, can you imagine, on your CV? *CV*, I thought, and felt a thrill of fear, the backwash of my desperation to have such a thing, to leave childhood and dependence behind me, to enter the world. There's some thyme here, I said, look, it would be good in the griddle cakes maybe, or if they do catch any fish.

They had caught fish, of course. It is only fair to observe that both Dad and the Prof did have the off-grid survival skills about which they liked to talk. When we got back, well after any conventional interpretation of 'lunch time', sunburnt and blue-fingered, our bags almost as flaccid as they had been that morning, a small school of silver

29

fish had been suffocated, disembowelled, opened out like pages and strung on a wooden frame to dry in the sun. There was a smell. You're back at last, said Dad, you know they wouldn't have gone off lazing around, summer was the busy time, they'd have known what would happen in winter if they couldn't be bothered to fill the stores. Is that really all you could find? And I dare say you're all expecting to eat regardless? They wouldn't have had two old men supplying the whole community you know, the young people would have played their part. Had to, I thought, seeing as how nobody actually lived to be old, seeing as how you and Prof Jim would have been dead and buried years ago, infection or appendicitis, parasites, the leg you broke that time you fell on the mountain. Sorry, said Dan, we did look, there just didn't seem to be much, maybe a different terrain next time, isn't moorland a man-made landscape anyway, from sheep-farming? The Prof was more relaxed. Never mind, he said, it's just an experiment, just to get a sense of the challenges. Here, Alison made flatbreads and there's lots of fish. Your bilberries should dry in no time, a day like today.

The basket-weaver came. What kind of job is that, said Mum, fancy making your living weaving baskets in this day and age, but it turned out, of course, to be more complicated than that. The baskets weren't to sell. Louise was a friend of the Prof, a semi-retired lecturer in textile arts who now spent her days making things by hand, the hard way, for the amusement of people bored by safe drinking water, modern medicine and dry feet. *Lecturer in Textile Arts*; I caught Dad's eye as he absented himself. She was wearing a sort of kaftan thing not unlike our tunics although probably more comfortable and certainly, even to my eye, more expensive, with lumpy flat shoes made of cut-out red leather flowers and green leaves sewn together. She'd driven her jeep up the track into the wood and then the Prof pushed her wheelchair up the field, a process that looked uncomfortable for both and unsafe for her but seemed to cause them great hilarity. Dan and Pete went to help but were waved away; thank you, she said, but Jim pushed me into Loch Lomond once upon a time, I'll see if I can trust him now. It was twenty-five years ago, he said. It was memorable, she said. Anyway, you must be Jim's students?

The Prof parked Louise's chair in the shade of the big oak and then went back with Pete to get her boxes of supplies from the car. Mum brought her a birchbark cup of water, offered tea she had no practical means of supplying. Don't worry, said Louise, the water is perfect and if I want tea later I have a tap and a perfectly good kettle at home. Oh, are you going? Do join us if you like, make a basket. Mum paused. Try it, said Louise, you can stop if it's not fun. It was the wrong word, Mum didn't believe in fun. I've a mort to do, she said, I'll be getting on, thank you. More water before I do?

The oak rustled, its shadows pattering over Louise's clothes and hair. I stood there, had nothing to say. Molly came through the sunlight, introduced herself and knelt at Louise's side, sitting on her flexed ankles in an elegant Japanese posture that I couldn't have managed. It's not easy to sit on the ground in a knee-length tunic. Either Ancient Britons worried a lot less about flashing their knickers than we do or the hunter-gatherer life made them very bendy. Not that they had knickers, probably. And this is Silvie, Molly said, Jim probably mentioned, Bill's daughter? Short for Sulevia. Hi, I said, feeling myself redden for no particular reason. Molly smiled at me, flicked a plait over her shoulder and started asking questions: don't you have to destroy an artefact to find out how it was made? Do you use replica tools to make replica objects, and if so do you use replica tools to make the replica tools, how far back does it go? Since the textiles themselves don't survive, how far are ideas about what people wore in prehistory just guess-work, these tunics, for example? I stood at the edge of the tree's shelter, leaves moving in my hair, wondering if she'd prepared these questions in advance, worrying that her rapid fire was rude. You don't talk to people like that, I thought, just come out and ask them stuff, but Molly did and Louise didn't seem to mind. Well, she said, a lot of archaeology is about taking things apart to see how they work, isn't it, and we often don't put them back when we've finished, but one of the reasons for making replicas is that you can test them to destruction if you need to. Sometimes I do use replica tools, I have quite a collection of bone needles at home, but you know sometimes you can use the real thing, there are enough medieval loom-weights and spindles around that we can put the real things in handling collections. Really, said Molly, you can spin using the very thing that someone, some woman, used before the Civil War? Doesn't it feel strange, I heard myself ask, putting your fingers exactly the way someone put hers only she's been dead for a few hundred years? Louise smiled, as if it was fine for me to join in. Not to me, she said, not any more, anyway,

I'm always trying to do what dead people tell me. And specially when I'm making a replica, spending days looking at and feeling and listening to some prehistoric object, I'm kind of trying to think their thoughts too. I mean, it would make sense, wouldn't it, that when I really concentrate on the spaces between decorative dots or the exact tension of a twist, my mind's doing what their minds did while my hands do what their hands did. I sometimes think I can tell when two pieces from the same site were made by the same prehistoric person, because the way my hands move is the same. I shivered. Of course, that was the whole point of the re-enactment, that we ourselves became the ghosts, learning to walk the land as they walked it two thousand years ago, to tend our fire as they tended theirs and hope that some of their thoughts, their way of understanding the world, would follow the dance of muscle and bone. To do it properly, I thought, we would almost have to absent ourselves from ourselves, leaving our actions, our re-enactions, to those no longer there. Who are the ghosts again, us or our dead? Maybe they imagined us first, maybe we were conjured out of the deep past by other minds.

It's a shame I couldn't bring a loom, Louise was

saying, it would have been interesting for you to see, perhaps I should ask Jim to arrange a session in my studio next term.

I turned out to have natural talent as a basket-weaver. Silvie's doing very well, said Louise, look at that, have you done this before, do you do a lot of making? Making what, I thought, but whatever she had in mind the answer was no. Great, I said to Moll, my future is settled, I'll weave baskets. Maybe not full time, Molly said, you must want to do something, there must be something you like, a starting point. I like reading, I said, but not what we do in English lessons. Um, going for walks? Nothing anyone'd pay me for. She pushed woven reeds down onto their willow frame. Mountain guiding, she said. Working in a youth hostel. Forestry and conservation. What about all the outdoor stuff, foraging, you know more about it than we do. Just the bilberries, I said, and only because of Dad, it wasn't as if there was any way I could not know that stuff, anyway I don't think it's a job.

Aviate, navigate, communicate, Dad always said, and don't expect that anyone will come and get you when it all goes wrong. I was pretty sure he'd never flown, nor even sat in a light aircraft; the aviation was metaphorical and what he meant by 'communicate' was 'don't ask for help'. I started to tuck the sticking-out ends into the weave of my basket. It was actually quite good, even and stable.

What about you, I said, you're going to be an archaeologist? Molly's plaits had come back to the front. There were green apples on them today. Maybe, she said, don't think I want to spend my life digging though, I like walls and a roof and a bathroom. I might go into museums and galleries, maybe do teacher training first so I can work with kids and families, I've always loved museums.

Museums. My father regarded them as temples, the bone-houses of our ancestral past. There wasn't much locally, just small-town collections going from the less exciting flint tools to patched hoop-skirts from someone's granny's attic, but my father was one of the few people who liked to go and look at them, and therefore to take me too. He had taken me once, years ago, to the Manchester Museum, told me I didn't need to go to school that day, we had better things to do, he and I. He'd told Mum to put up sandwiches for us, sent me back upstairs to take off my uniform and put on 'summat decent', and then sent me back to change again when I, matching his one suit with the wide legs, came down in my party dress.

Come on, he said, we don't want to miss the train. I had never been on the train. We held hands and I trotted, as always, to keep up with him, past the butcher where the pork and lamb and beef in the window were divided from each other like the animals on the toy farm at school by plastic grass, past the Post Office where I went with Mum every Thursday straight after school to pick up the Child Benefit and we queued on the dusty lino floor around the metal barriers, because Thursday was also the day you collected your pension so there were old ladies with sweets in their handbags for little girls who knew how to be winsome, which I didn't, mostly. Dad strode up the cobbled lane to the station, bought tickets, told me to stay behind the yellow line on the platform and not to act daft. It was only on the train that he started to explain where we were going, as I pressed my nose to the grimy window and took in the marine tartan of British Rail, poked my fingers into what turned out to be ash-trays in the arm of each seat. Stop that, he said, listen now. I knew about the peat bogs up on the moor, yes, the ones where the cotton flags grew, where we had to jump from tussock to tussock not to fall in the mire? Even then, when I must have slowed him down enough to be annoying, he took me walking up there every Sunday, whatever the weather;

yes, I knew. Right, well those bogs have always been special places for folk round here, right back in ancient times, people saw the marshlights, probably, thought it was spirits or summat like, and probably they were frightened to fall in just like us because I knew, didn't I, that the bog could hold you down and suck you in, he'd told me, hadn't he, how hard it could be to get out. Aye, I said, yes. We were crossing the moor by then, the wires swooping along the tracks, and it was a clear enough grey day but I couldn't see any bog, just heather and sheep and below us terraced houses like our own creeping up the hillside. Well, he said, folk used sometimes to give their precious things to the bog, like if you were to give it your Owl. In my mind I clasped Owl tightly, sent a thought to him left undefended in my bed, tried not to imagine his fur darkening as he sank, the bog swallowing his yellow felt feet. Or if you gave it your digging books, I said. There was a bookshelf for Dad's digging books, by the gas fire in the front room. Mum couldn't watch TV unless Dad was working a night shift because he liked to read them there in the evenings, in silence, and although I wasn't allowed to touch them he'd sometimes show me the pictures when I came down to say goodnight. These are Bronze Age necklaces, Silvie, can you imagine how heavy to wear? That's a sword, look at that inlay, think of the work in that. And on this rock, look, they carved a magic pattern, someone did that by hand three thousand years since. That's where you come from, those folk, that's how it used to be. I looked round and saw him tense at the thought of throwing his big shiny books in a bog. Ripped pages, spreading water. Aye, I suppose, he said, but you know you're not to touch them mind. Anyroad, there's been all sorts found in the bogs, the peat and the water preserve stuff that rots away everywhere else and of course there's always been digging for peats so things get found. And Silvie, out Cheshire way they found a person, a man. From the really old days, the Iron Age. A man, I said, what, dead? Of course dead, you lummock, didn't I just say Iron Age, when was the Iron Age? I knew that one. Two thousand years, I said, before the Romans came. Well, there you go then, he's not going to be alive, is he. We were coming to the next station. The people who wanted to get off had to push the windows all the way down and lean out to use the handle on the outside of the door. Did he fall in then, I asked, get sucked down? Pushed in, more like, said Dad, and a rope round his neck and all. You're going to see him, Silvie, today. They've got him all laid out in a case at the museum. A real man from the Iron Age, himself. But dead, I said again, unable to imagine it.

My dad likes museums, I said to Molly. He likes dead things. She pulled a strand out of her basket and started winding it around the spokes again. I'd like to make things be alive again, she said, like Louise does, let visitors see that people's tools and jewellery and games are still here even when the people aren't. And I wish I was better at this, I like the idea of making things the way people used to. Practice, I said, I bet the baskets in museums weren't anyone's first attempt.

Though some of the bog bodies must have been someone's first attempt. It would have been a skill to learn like any other, the art of taking someone into the flickering moment between life and death and holding them there, gone and yet speaking, moving still, for as long as you liked.

There were cold bannocks for the meal we called tea and the Prof called dinner, with greens Dad had found while we were weaving baskets and more of the fish, which were lasting well partly because they were so small and bony that only Dad had the patience for more than one. Half a bannock left lumpen on my plate, I watched him

40

use his fingers to work flakes of pale flesh from skin and bone and then suck on the heads, shrunken eyes open to his tongue and teeth. What, he said, picking his teeth with a fingernail, summat bothering you, not enough refinement round here for you? No, I said, nothing. Good, he said, they wouldn't have wasted food you know, wouldn't have left what could be eaten. And nor will you, eat the bannock your mother made now. I saw him looking at Molly's plate; she'd refused fish and only tasted the greens. You don't go wasting what people have worked for, he said, but into the air between me and her. No Dad, I said, and afterwards, when the others went off up the hill to see the sunset, he made me stay and help Mum, wipe weird bowls and rough wooden spoons with bunches of reeds he'd told her to gather earlier, then rinse them in the stream. Bits of fish caught in the reeds. He wouldn't have a dishwasher at home, said they wasted water and it was good for folk to clean up after themselves with their own two hands, but there was a washing-up ritual that he supervised for months before he trusted me alone: scrape into the compost bucket, hot water rinse, soap scrub, second rinse, dry with a fresh cloth, put away. Can't abide to see dishes left all heaped, how can you clean the sink if it's like that. Even when we went camping, we had tin plates and after I'd rinsed them in the stream they got a proper wash in water heated over a driftwood fire. Won't we get sick, I said, why don't we just eat off leaves and then throw them away? I suppose they didn't get sick, Mum said, the whojamacallits. Ancient Britons. We'd have to wash the leaves first, anyroad, and I can't think of big ones that aren't poisonous. They might well have got food poisoning, I said, something was keeping life expectancy down, the Professor said in most cases they didn't even live long enough to die of cancer. Oh well, she said. There was a new bruise on her arm. Here, she said, put these back in the hut and then maybe we can sit down a bit before bedtime. Mum often spoke of sitting down as a goal, a prize she might win by hard work, but so rarely achieved that the appeal remained unclear to me. She worked as a cashier for the local supermarket, a job mostly conducted from a seat but apparently not meeting whatever need was meant by 'sitting down'. You go now, I said, you go sit down, I'll sort these last bits. I carried the bowls and spoons down to the stream, plopped them into a pool where the water eddied smooth and deep and left them to rinse a bit. I meandered in the evening light, feeling heather and stones under my feet, breathing the smell of leaves and dew. I slapped at midges, picked a few clover leaves and watched them shimmy away on the stream into the dimming evening, dipped my fingers and admired the way the water distorted their lines. A few dark fish ghosted the pool. I saw a bog myrtle bush leaning over the water downstream, pewter leaved, and picked my way towards it, rubbed a leaf between my fingers and inhaled the scent of eucalyptus and sandalwood. I squatted for a little while on the bank and listened to the sounds of the night, no birds now but the stream hurrying over stones it had worn to roundness, small lives rustling somewhere within reach, a distant owl and a nearer response. I didn't leave until it occurred to me that I was going to have trouble carrying everything back to the camp in the dark, although I found I could see well enough until I came within sight of the fire. Light blinds you; there's a lot you miss by gathering at the fireside.

The students were still not back, although by any measure sunset was gone. Dad and the Prof were talking about fighting, the way men do when they're really fighting about talking. It would just have been intertribal squabbles up here, the Prof was saying, until the Romans came, no training at all for taking on the imperial army, they'd never have seen the like. At least part of their defence was magic, did you know that? War trumpets, scary noises coming at you over the marsh. Aye, said Dad, maybe so, you're thinking of the carnyxes, but they had their horses and swords as well, didn't they, put up quite a fight and after all sent them packing in the end, there weren't dark faces in these parts for nigh on two millennia after that, were there? Carnyces, said the Prof, in the plural, and hang on, we don't— And anyway, I said, don't the Americans use magic and scary noises to this day, don't they paint pictures on their bombs and play heavy metal outside their enemies' compounds? Dad looked at the Prof as if I were his second-in-command, as if I'd just backed him up as planned. Yes, said the Prof, they do, and you're right, it's probably very much the same thing; one of the things you learn in my line of work is that there's no steady increase in rationalism over the centuries, it's a mistake to think that they had primitive minds and we don't. The Britons had enough training that the Romans had to build the Wall, Dad said, they wouldn't have bothered with that, would they, if the British hadn't put the wind up them. Well, said the Prof, they weren't exactly British, as I said before, they wouldn't have seen themselves that way, as far as we can tell their identities were tribal. Celts, we tend to call them these days though they wouldn't have recognized the idea, they seem to have come from Brittany and Ireland, from the West. Dad didn't like this line. Celts, I suppose, sounded Irish, and even though Jesus had only recently died at the time in question Dad didn't like the Irish, tended to see Catholicism in much the same light as the earlier form of Roman imperialism. Foreigners coming over here, telling us what to think. He wanted his own ancestry, wanted a lineage, a claim on something. Not people from Ireland or Rome or Germania or Syria but some tribe sprung from English soil like mushrooms in the night. What about Boadicea, Dad said, she routed them an' all, didn't she. Boudicca, said the Prof, we call her Boudicca these days, it seems to be a more accurate rendition. For a while, yes, but she led the Iceni in the south, there's not much evidence that the people round here caused the Romans any major alarm, the Wall was much more of a symbol than a military necessity.

Mum, sitting on a rock a little behind him, was gazing at her own hands. I guessed this didn't count as sitting down, that she wanted her brown velvet armchair and the telly instead of woodsmoke and talk about the Iron Age.

But – said Dad. You can see, said the Prof, think about the stretch along Whin Sill, you've already got a bloody great escarpment running for miles, no possible need to stick a wall on top, doesn't make it any harder to cross or any easier to police, it's just a very impressive way of saying Rome Was Here. Yeah, said Dad, OK, but what about – Mum tensed. Her glance flickered towards him and away. It's a marker, said Prof Slade, the edge of empire, it's not to keep the barbarians out so much as to show where they are. It was never the Berlin Wall, Bill, no raked earth or watchtowers. Dad didn't say anything. He lifted his chin, locked eyes with the fire. Mum hunched on her rock, touched her arm where I'd seen the bruise earlier.

Dad was already up and gone by the time I woke up the next morning. Mum was outside stirring gruel again; Dan and Pete had managed to set up a kind of stone trivet for her so she was standing at the fireside and there was steam rising from the pot. Her cheeks were flushed. Those stones'll explode, I said, if they heat unevenly, and they will because one side's obviously going to get hotter than the other. Happen, she said. But Mum, I said, if it does happen you'll get hurt. She shrugged. Aye. Mum, I said, it's not safe. She stirred her pot. Folk have been building stone fireplaces a long time, Silvie, I daresay they know what they were about. Yeah, I said, but that doesn't mean those lads know what they're about, does it? Give over, she said. All right, but why don't you let someone else do some cooking, have a break, I could manage, or Molly. Oh, she said, I don't mind, I'd rather eat my own cooking than whatever those students might come up with, and you know I'm not one for rambling, never was. I wondered again what my parents had ever had in common. OK, I said, if you're happy, it just doesn't seem very fair, that's all. Life isn't, she said, which was what she always said. Mustn't grumble, can't be helped, nothing to be gained by making a fuss, well, you wouldn't want to make trouble, would you?

Dad and the Prof came back while the guys were eating their breakfast and Mum, Molly and I were pushing ours around. Gruel is a thing you can eat without thinking about it as long as you're very hungry, a bit like white sauce or maybe wallpaper paste. It was the first time I'd seen the boys eat like that and I was impressed. Have mine, I said, really, I'm not very hungry. Mum, are there any of those bannock things left? No, she said, and someone's going to have to grind some grain if you want more of them for lunch. Or we could just get sandwiches from Spar, said Molly, and grinned at me while the boys started explaining to her why we couldn't. They were so loud we didn't hear the bushes rustling and Dad came out saying, what, what's this about Spar? Just a joke, said Mum, Molly was just teasing, have you two had a good time? We weren't off on a jolly, said Dad, don't talk to me as if I were some kid. Setting traps for rabbits, said the Prof, they count as vermin so it's legal. Not quite authentic of course, they were introduced by the Romans, but it's something. No, said Molly, not spring traps, they're cruel. I was waiting for Dad to say life is cruel, get used to it, you'll be happy enough to eat a stew. Not spring traps, said the Prof, they wouldn't have had them. Don't worry about it, Molly, you don't need to know, we won't make you deal with them if you don't want to, but you know they would have killed animals, it would have been as ordinary as going to the shops, death would have been part of their daily normality in a way that we can't imagine. They'd have brought the kill home and it would have been like getting back from the supermarket, unpacking, take the skin to scrape and the bones for tools, wind the sinews for sewing leather and blow up the bladder for the children to play ball. Some bloody supermarket he's got there, murmured Dan, don't fancy the scene in his kitchen. Molly had put down her bowl. Yeah, she said, well, whatever, I'm happy to leave it at the imagining stage, poor old rabbits.

I could see Mum wanting to ask Dad to wash his hands before eating but she didn't. He ate fast, blindly, his gaze fixed on something near his feet. She watched him. The Prof waved his spoon around a lot and went on talking, Iron Age hunting techniques, flint knapping, someone he knew who'd nearly lost an eye which was why he himself had always been meticulous about goggles, how he thought Iron Age flint knappers might have protected their eyes, evidence for very early forms of surgery and suturing. The shadows were already shorter and sharper than they had been when I got up, the beginnings of another hot day. We were wearing a path between the hut, the fireplace and the tents, and all the rabbit droppings were turning pale and dry. We must have dispossessed the rabbits, and who knew what birds and voles, with our talking and coming and going and our fire. Right, said the Prof, so Silvie, you'll go with Molly and the lads? He didn't have the right kind of accent to say 'lads'. Er, sure,

I said, go where? Jesus, Silvie, said Dad, you haven't been listening to a single word, have you?

We went to the beach. This time the Prof checked that we had the foraging book and knew where to look for edible seaweed and mussels. Low tide, he said, late morning, and I checked before we came that that beach is clean, we could have a real feast this evening. There's wild garlic, I said, at the edge of the wood. We often ate mussels while camping, but Dad always resisted the garlic. Hungry folk want plain food, he said, the corollary being that if you didn't want 'plain food' you weren't hungry and so shouldn't be eating in the first place. Good idea, said the Prof, we can eat the greens as well. See you later, enjoy yourselves. I don't think he minded at all that the students were having more fun than we could reasonably assume the Iron Age community had enjoyed. I don't think he'd have minded much about the fruit pastilles.

The others had been going to the beach on their day trips last term and walked briskly at first. There was no path. The sun was too bright in my eyes and already I could feel the skin on my forearms beginning to burn. How far is it, I asked. Half an hour, said Pete, why, you tired? What's it like sleeping in the hut? Dark, I said.

Very dark, even in the mornings. And we can hear each other breathe, all night, there's no privacy. What about the beds, said Dan, are they really lumpy? Don't think so, I said, not that I've noticed. Mum says they're doing her back in. Dad had been scornful about Mum's back. Try getting a bit more exercise, he said, we weren't never meant to spend our lives sat on our backsides, and no wonder folk have trouble the amount of time they spend sat on them sofas. We did not have a sofa, and Mum's armchair was one her mother's friend Eileen had discarded as worn out. What's it like in the tents, I asked, although I knew perfectly well what it is like in a tent. Cramped and stuffy, said Molly, and light all the time, I keep waking up about when I'd normally be going to sleep at the weekend, I see why they built huts. Swap, I said, you listen to my dad snoring all night and I'll get up early. Yeah, she said, thanks, no deal.

The next field had cows in it. No way, said Molly, they weren't here last time, I'm not going through there. Mostly when cows kill folk, I said, it's because someone's dogs have bothered the cows, they don't just attack innocent bystanders, you know they're herbivores. I don't care, she said, I'm not going into that field. You can walk in the middle, said Dan, we'll protect you, they'll have to trample our bodies into the mud to get you. Nope, she said, not happening. So there were some barbed-wire fences to negotiate, which is harder to do in a linen tunic than in jeans, and then a river, which meant a diversion through the sand dunes where it is remarkably easy to get lost even when you know the sun is in the south-east and you are on the east coast and that means as long as the sun is in both your eyes but bothering the right one more you will soon come to the water. You're so good at this stuff, Silvie, said Molly, I suppose your dad taught you. No, I thought, I just know the approximate shape of this island and that the sun rises in the east and I didn't need to be taught either of those things, but I said mm, it's his kind of thing. Jesus it's hot, said Dan, does anyone have any water? Can we stop in the shade for a bit? Molly, of course, had a plastic bottle of cola, warm and unpleasantly sticky, though by then even the west side of the dunes had no shade. We've actually managed to lose the sea, said Pete, can you imagine what Silvie's dad's going to say when we explain that there aren't any mussels because we couldn't find the coast? Molly giggled. I stood up and slithered through the sand and sharp marram grass to the top of the dune. I can see it, I said, funnily enough we just keep heading east, it hasn't moved. I'm so hot, said Dan, the first thing I'm going to do when we get there is swim. The tide's out, I said, the first thing you'll have to do is walk about half a mile to the water, and even before he replied I wished I hadn't said it. Know-it-all. OK, he said, rub it in why don't you.

When we came to the beach it looked more like a desert, the sea itself a fiction on the horizon. We all took off our moccasins as soon as we were past the last of the sharp grass. Mine were wearing through. Molly's toenails were painted sparkly blue. I was intrigued to see that Dan's feet were even hairier than his legs; Dad's were the only male feet I knew and they were as smooth as mine. Without talking about it we headed straight out towards the sea, towards the place where the hot sand began to cool and to ripple under our feet. At the edges of the bay I could see rocks where there would be mussels. Later, I thought, mussels and seaweed, I don't think you get samphire on a beach like this. Not now. Our shadows on the sand were those of the Iron Age, and I remembered Doggerland, the name archaeologists gave the human settlements now under the North Sea. Once people had chased deer across this land, had camped, had carved figurines in bone and wood, in taking off their clothes dropped brooches and buttons which had not moved when the sea came creeping, when the tide rose and did not turn. You used to be able to walk from the marshy lowlands of Denmark to the Northumbrian forest. You used to have stones and grass under your soles all the way.

Around us the earth flattened out, the green detail of the land receding although we were still on it, out on England's blurred margins. You'd think a coastline more definite than a land border but it's not so, not when you walk the watery edge at the turn of the tide and cannot say if you are on dry land, exactly. Do you know, said Dan, the British coast gets longer the more you measure it? We tried one day in the first year, they brought us to the beach and gave us tasks and questions and that was one of them, measure the shoreline, and of course the harder you try the more of it there is, round the rock pools and up and down every slope and after a while we realised it's infinite, the edge of an island is infinite. I suppose that was the point. It wasn't much of a point, said Molly, and as I recall it was bloody cold and there was nowhere for the girls to pee. No poetry in your soul, said Dan, that's the problem with girls, they're always thinking about where to pee. Molly kicked water out of a rock-pool at him and I said, my voice coming out surprisingly high, so would you be thinking about where to pee if you had to squat with your trousers round your ankles every time. It was one of my father's themes, the way women allow their inferior plumbing to shape their relationship with the Great Outdoors. Actually, said Molly, it's no harder for girls to pee than boys, the problem isn't biology, it's men's fear of women's bodies. If we were allowed to pull our knickers down and squat by a wall the way you're allowed to get your dick out and piss up the wall there wouldn't be a problem, it's just the way you all act as if a vagina will come and eat you if it's out without a muzzle. Hey, joke, Dan said, I was joking, don't get upset. That's the problem with boys, said Molly, they're always telling people not to get upset. Vagina, I thought, she just said the word out loud. In front of boys. Children, children, said Pete, do you think the sea's actually out there or are we just walking to Norway? Denmark, I said, actually, and it's too hot, this isn't a beach it's a desert, the mussels are going to be cooked before we ever get to them.

We came at last to the water, to waves smoothing themselves over paper-flat sand. Further out, much further out, there was rising and falling like breathing and white sunlight flashing out but no breaking, no crash.

Looks as if you'd have to go miles for a swim, said Dan. I kept going into the water, which at first was warm as blood. Feet, ankles, calves. I hiked up my tunic. Take it off, said Molly. Here, I'm going to. There was nowhere to leave a garment, nowhere dry for a long way. Don't suppose it matters if it gets wet, I said, but Molly had handed her bag to Pete and pulled her tunic over her head. Her bra and matching pants were the purple of chocolate wrappers, and there was pale hair poking through the lace of the pants, uncontainable. Her belly was rounder than mine, a pale curve dented by her belly button. I suddenly wanted to touch. I looked away. She splashed past me. Dan and Pete looked unconcerned, as if they saw women half-naked in public every day, but I saw Pete glancing away and then back and then away again. Molly, up to her waist, reached round to unhook her bra from behind in a way I'd seen on TV though not, for example, in the girls' changing room. She threw it to Dan, who fumbled, caught a strap, stood there with it dangling from his finger. Careful with that, I thought, can't have been cheap, matching and all. She pushed her shoulders back, closed her eyes and lifted her face to the sky, as if offering her breasts to the sun. Bigger than mine, smaller nipples, already an outdoor colour; she had done this before. She opened her eyes and looked back at us, watching her. Come on, she said, you all said you were too hot. Come on in, the water's lovely. We get the message, Moll, Dan said, you're gorgeous, nice tits. As if it was mildly tiresome of her to undress for us, as if it was boring to look. He yawned. Yeah, all right, why not, he said.

Male bodies, Dan's furred with dark hair, a thicker seam straight down from his navel, Pete bare as a piglet. Boxer shorts. A pink mushroom peeping at Pete's thigh. I remembered whispers from girls at school, it were *that big*, though my own fumblings in the park with Simon from the year above had been strictly above the waist and not, really, apart from the novelty of the thing, very exciting. It was Molly I watched, Molly's breasts lifting and falling as she jumped what waves there were, water beading on the curve of Molly's shoulders, trickling down the narrow pathway of her spine between the plaits dark with the North Sea. Dan and Pete splashed her, leapt away, egged each other out into deeper water.

I stood there, thigh deep, feeling the small wash of waves against my knees and the heat of the sun hammering my back and head, an armful of coarse brown cloth clasped to my chest while the three older and braver than me disported themselves.

It got hotter. The tide must have turned but it seemed that nothing was moving, that our walking back towards the land made no difference to where we were. Sand ground between my toes, clung to the down on my legs. I could feel it beneath my fingernails, in the damp under my arms. I licked sweat off my upper lip and had sand on my tongue and between my teeth. The beach underfoot had hardened in ridges, like walking over bones. My head ached. We went in single file, Dan then Pete then Molly then me, feet following step after step, step after step. Water, I kept thinking, water, but I knew we didn't have any. I chewed on my tongue to make my mouth water but it didn't work. I could feel my heartbeat in my head, thick blood thudding against my skull, behind my eyes. There was a stream at the end of the dunes, unbelievable as a happy ending. We kept going.

We returned to the camp mid-afternoon, our two bags of mussels already giving off a worse than fishy smell. These bags are going to stink, said Molly, hefting them over a stile, we'll all get ill, though I suppose then we can go back to the world of indoor plumbing and ice-cream. Dan caught my eye. Girls and toilets, he murmured, what did I tell you?

Mum came out of the hut as we arrived. I thought she had been sleeping, or maybe crying; she had a private look on her face and could barely open her eyes in the sunlight. There you are, she said pointlessly. I'm going to the stream, I said, I'm all hot and sandy and I need water. Molly had folded in the shade of the big oak, lain back and closed her eyes. Don't drink the stream water, Mum said, here, there's spring water in the jug.

I couldn't bear to put my feet back into the wet sandy moccasins and picked my way barefoot down to the stream. I had imagined I might bathe in it, had perhaps seen myself reclining like Ophelia, hair flowing, but of course it was far too shallow. I glanced around, took off the sweaty, sand-crusted tunic and left it in a heap on the grass. I remembered Molly's purple lace and looked down at my washed-out, once-white cotton pants and a bra whose 'flesh tone' might have been convincing on a trout. It won't show through your school shirts, Mum had said. When I grow up, I thought, when I get away, I will go out and buy myself pants in emerald and turquoise and scarlet and I will wear them with bras that are orange and lime and what Mum calls shocking pink. I will have lipstick and thin tights and high heels, I will have cowboy boots like Claire's Aunty Sue. I stepped into the stream, balancing on the stones. The moorland water was colder than the sea had been, its pull faster. I turned and waded upstream, remembering a peaty amber pool up past the rowans. A breeze came down from the moor and breathed on my belly and chest. I kept slipping on slimy rocks, knew the water wasn't deep enough to cushion a fall. If I knocked my head, I thought, I would lie here and drown, they would find me in my wet undies, blood wavering like weed, but I kept going, my mind now full of the image of myself sitting in the pool which had become rounded and deep, dappled with leaf-shade, where my arms could lift and float tanned by the rusty water.

When I got to the place I'd remembered it was barely knee-deep and not particularly near any trees, and the water so dark I couldn't see what I was sitting on as I lowered myself, but I sat there anyway in oozy mud, the roots of long-dead trees poking my bottom, knees sticking up with the waterline below my navel. I tilted back uncomfortably, the pool not wide enough for me to lean, but the water stroked my sunburn, soothed away the itchy sand. I crossed my legs, tucked my feet under my thighs where the mud was slick and cool, felt cold water filter through my knickers and right inside me. I looked around again and struggled to undo my bra the way Molly had undone hers, hands behind my shoulders, let it lift away from my shoulder blades, felt my nipples harden like hers as I leant forward and dipped them in the cold marsh water. I touched them, watched the shape of my breasts change. I splashed my face, closed my eyes and saw my blood's rose-red in the sun. I thought then about what might be around me, folded in the peat, what other limbs might be held in the same dark water, what other eyes closed, and that's where I was when Dad and the Prof came striding over the heather. They were carrying dead rabbits hanging from strings tied around the back legs, the mouths dribbling blood onto the turf and haloed with flies. The water wasn't deep enough to hide in, not even to cover my breasts which were after all barely large enough to qualify, and though I scrabbled with the bra straps behind my back I was too late, couldn't do it. Dad apologised to the Prof, maybe the second time I'd heard him apologise to anyone ever, and sent him on. When he'd gone, Dad put down his rabbits – their eyes still bright, I noticed, and no obvious traumatic injuries – and hauled me out of the water which he didn't need to do, I would have got out when he told me to. Cover yourself, he said, eyes averted in disgust, where are your clothes, and with a hand twisted through my hair dragged me stumbling through the heather and reeds back to where the tunic lay in the sun. Put it on, he said, you should be ashamed of yourself, I'll not have my daughter a little whore, and only when I had covered myself and turned back to face him did he take off his Iron Age leather belt. Stand against that tree, he said, a rowan not much taller than me, the trunk against which I leant my forehead no wider than my face, and as his arm rose and swung and rose again, as the belt sang through the sunny air, I thought hard about the tree between my hands, about the cells in its leaves photosynthesizing the afternoon sun, about the berries ripening hour by hour, the impalpable pulse of sap under my palms, the reach of roots below my feet and deep into the earth. It went on longer than usual, as if the open air invigorated him, as if he liked the setting. I thought about the leather of his belt, the animal from whose skin it was made, about the sensations that skin had known before the fear and pain of the end. Itching, scratching, wind and rain and sun. About the flaying, the tanning. Pick up those rabbits, he said when he had finished, and don't let me ever catch you stripping again, lying around naked like that, waiting for one of those lads I'd say, and don't you imagine I won't do this again as often as it takes, as long as you're living under my roof you'll behave yourself or else, do you understand. The belt swung from his hand. What are you standing there for, did I not just tell you to get the rabbits, are you wanting more, believe me you can have it if you are.

I walked ahead of him back to the hut, the rabbits on their string held at arm's length. Their heads lolled, but the ears were still laid back. If there was a smell, it was faint, more of fur and digested grass than of blood. Hang them up by the fish, he said, you'll gut them later, you and your friends. Now help your mother with the cooking, I daresay she's behind again and folk hungry.

She was 'behind', and everyone else was sitting in the shade with cups of water. Well, she said, we don't want anyone getting sunstroke and you've brought us a fair lot of mussels, I've had Molly put them in the stream, we'll eat them later for dinner, the problem with these flatbread things, bannocks or what-have-you, you have to do them one at a time, see, can't put a whole batch in the oven, folk'll just have to wait a bit but your father won't like it, the dough's there, see, if you can shape a few more I'll see to these in the pan. Griddle, I mean, or whatever he calls it. OK, I said, what, about this size? Ah Silvie, she said, you've upset him again, haven't you? What, I said, how do you know, what do you mean. I can tell, she said, I am your mum, what was it this time? Nothing, I said, it doesn't matter, it's over now, you know what he's like, it'll all be fine for a few days now. I just wish you wouldn't provoke him, she said, if you didn't wind him up all the time he wouldn't do it. I know, I said, I didn't mean to, sometimes I do mean to but this time I didn't. Well, she said, just don't do it again, whatever it was, there's enough here already mithering him.

Dad made us butcher the rabbits after lunch. Or at least, once we'd eaten; it was probably too late to be lunch. It will be interesting, the Prof said, to see how the flint knives work, they're certainly sharp enough. Molly, could you bring the basket, please? Molly stood up. Sunburn was beginning to flame across her nose and cheeks. I'll bring the basket, she said, sure, but I'm not cutting open any rabbits, I'm not even going to watch. Oh, said Dad, but I suppose you'll eat them when someone else has done the dirty work, I suppose you're not actually a vegetarian? Fine, she said, I am now, if that's what it takes. It's all right, Molly, said the Prof, we don't need everyone to do everything, why don't you help Alison, wash the cups or whatever. I'm going to wash some clothes, Molly said, this tunic's horrible. Mum, I said, would you mind doing mine for me, if I'm cutting up rabbits, I got so hot on the beach, it's all sandy. All right, she said, give it here, and what about you lads, if we're doing three we might as well do six, not that I'm expecting much without proper soap but we can freshen them up and it's a good drying day for sure.

I went into the hut, knelt on my bunk where no-one could see, and took off the tunic. Even if there had been light, the tender places on my skin were of course at the back, not where I could see, but I ran my fingertips over what I could reach, mapped skin with skin. It was bad. It was a shame, I thought, things hadn't happened the other way around, the belt before the stream, because the cold water would have helped me now. Although of course if I hadn't gone into the stream in the first place I probably wouldn't have needed cold water. Unless he'd found some other reason; some days I just knew he needed to hit me and however carefully I trod, sooner or later I'd give him cause, but this time I thought it really was what I'd done that had made him angry. I should have known, I thought, I should have gone further away, I should have kept my bra on, he wasn't wrong about that, and what if one of the boys had come along? The flap over the door opened. Mum, outlined against the sky. Are you all right in there, Silvie, only your dad's asking for you, please don't keep him waiting now. I'm fine, I said, I'm coming, just a minute.

You start by peeling off the rabbit's skin. Cut off the paws, Dad said, like this, and run the blade around here. Slice along the leg. Bring this cut to join it. Up the middle of the belly, usually you'd go around the neck but since we're planning to use the skins we'll go up like this. Do the forelegs. Then it's easy, peel it like a banana. Might have to tug a bit, mind. Then you can cut the head off at the end, easier with a metal blade for that, see, to get through the spine. I'd seen him do it before, albeit with kitchen shears and what he called his 'hunting knife', as if we lived somewhere where men were regularly dismembering animals in the course of daily life, like the American frontier in the nineteenth century or, I suppose, Iron Age Northumberland, but the boys were visibly shaken. What was that, Dan? said Dad. Dan shook his head but I'd heard him: I'm not gonna puke, I'm not gonna puke, think about Gran's roses. There was blood now, all right, and the smell of it. You'd think that dismembering something would get easier as the creature becomes less like itself, but with rabbits that's not the case: a skinned rabbit looks disturbingly similar to a decapitated baby. Or so I imagine. OK, said Dad, then you just slit up the belly and pull out the guts. Intestines, see, lungs and heart, think that one's the liver.

I watched Dad's hands. Skin, I thought, his skin and my skin, the tanned skin of his belt, the soft furred skin of the rabbit, our surfaces, our barrier between blood and air. Water can't get further than skin, unless it's bog water in which case it will permeate skin and preserve it like leather forever, so that the surface outlasts brain and blood by two thousand years. Leather shoes, to protect living skin. Leather belts, to make it sore. Dad's fingers, dark with blood, dropped the rabbit's innards on the grass.

Dan puked.

Oh dear, said Dad, it's usually the ladies being squeamish, isn't it, you'd think a lad'd have more guts. So to speak. Right, so that's how you do it. We can joint them later if that's what Alison wants, have to see how she's going to cook them. OK, you lot get to work on those. Silvie, don't forget to pick up the lights.

Dad left. Dan tried to scrabble leaves over where he'd been sick. The smell rose in the sunshine. It's all right, said Pete, sit down a bit. Jesus. Nearly vommed myself.

67

He glanced at me. Is he always like that, Silvie? I mean, sorry, I know he's your dad and all but. Like what, I said, a show-off and given to brutality, yes, actually, mostly he is, sorry. I could see Dan and Pete exchanging glances, almost see the words cross the air between us: what is he like to live with then, how is your home and your life? So've you done this before, Dan asked, with the rabbits? I've helped him do it, I said, though not with stone tools. I think it gets easier but anyway we're going to have to do it, aren't we, so we might as well get started. I picked up a blade and a rabbit. It was only the heat of the day, of course, that made the rabbit still warm, that gave the impression that I was hacking at the paws of a living being. It was not flinching, only springing back as I cut through nerves, scraped on bone. The eyes were beginning to dull. I still didn't know how the men had killed them.

Inevitably it was hard to sleep that night. Without a proper pillow I couldn't lie on my front without twisting my neck too hard, and Dad must have done some backhand or changed hands so the belt had wrapped around both sides; the tree thoughts had worked and I hadn't noticed at the time, but he always liked symmetry.

It hurt to lie on either side as well as on my back. I thought of the tree, the smooth pale bark under my palms, warm to my forehead. Rowans were often planted at doorways and boundaries, meant to deter evil spirits or maybe to invite good ones, I couldn't recall. You find them often by the ruins of old cottages up on the moors. I pushed up onto my hands and knees on my straw sack, let my head hang down to ease my neck. Evil spirits, I thought, ghosts, like the bog people Dad loved who could now exist only as victims, as the objects of violence. There had been a new book out the previous year, one with colour photographs. She was a young teenager, Dad had said, about your age they think, though she was small and she'd have walked funny, she was crippled. Looks as if she'd had rough treatment for a good while, when they X-rayed her they found all sorts of old fractures that had healed up before death. How do you think she died, Silvie? He'd pushed the photo in front of me, the bones of arms and legs coming through the skin, leathered torso fallen over ribcage and pelvis, but an expression still, just about, on her bog-tanned face, long hair still braided as she must have braided it that last morning. Eyelids, still, eyelashes, over empty sockets. The rope around her neck, I said, she was strangled, but of course I knew that the bog people rarely had only one way to die. Aye, he said, mebbe, at the end, but could be she was still alive when she went in, this one was staked, look, through the upper arms, those holes are where the sticks went, seems they cut off that foot too though no knowing if that were before or after death, also there was a proper blow to the head, look, here on the next page. And these cuts here, they were before death. He looked up at me, touched my forearm in its school uniform shirt and my shoulder. They'd be about there and there, see, not enough to kill, just done for the pain like, and this one on her face, there, for the shame of it maybe, folk watching. My forehead, along the hairline. Yes, I said, I see. Her hands had been bound for two thousand years.

I lay down again in my bunk. She had had a life before that, the bog-girl. She had slept and woken, had sleepless nights, felt sun and wind and rain. She had learnt to read the sky, learnt the impossible dance of fingers plaiting her own hair behind her head, the movements just the same as the ones I'd been watching Molly make. There are few bog-children and so far as I know no bog-babies, so the people who come to us now out of the bogs must have been cared for, fed, must have been part of their families and villages until one day they found that they were no longer like everyone else, that sometime in the night something had changed. No-one knows how far before death that day might have been, whether one morning someone came to wake you carrying a rope, the blades already sharpened and waiting in the heather, or whether you had weeks or months to say your farewells, to get used to your status as a ghost. It would have been necessary not to think about it, I thought, to have tree-thoughts right to the end of thinking, and I found myself hoping they had something to hold, some talisman against the pain.

I knew they did not.

As the birdsong outside got louder I gave up, stifled a squeak as I rolled out of bed and trod cautiously towards the doorway. If he woke, I thought, if he caught me, he would either be pleased by my early rising, maybe even offer a moment of dawn companionship of the sort we had often shared when I was little and sometimes already up and playing quietly downstairs when he came in from a night-shift, or he would accuse me of sneaking around at night and get angry again. I ducked under the flap in the doorway and waited a moment – I could, after all, be going into the wood to pee, or getting a drink of water. Without a house, it occurred to me, it is much harder to restrict a person's movement. Harder for a man to restrain a woman.

There was a light mist tangled in the trees and the sun still too low for shadows. The sky was pale, branches vague against it. I stepped into cold grass wet with dew and my sunburnt feet liked it. I wrapped my arms around myself and took a deep breath of cool air that smelt of green things growing. Birdsong, something high and excitable in a nearby bush and the blackbird I'd heard yesterday in the oak tree. No wind, the dawn still. I thought briefly, lightly, of going back to the water, but I knew I wouldn't. Up onto the moor, I thought, sunrise, why not, although I knew that there's nowhere to hide up there, that if he woke and came that way, after more rabbits perhaps, he would see me anywhere within a five-mile radius, even if that also meant he would see that I was alone and not consorting with men. Albeit in my pyjamas. Pyjamas might be half-naked. I shouldn't be out here. My thoughts were beginning to flicker, my mind a bird against the window. It was often like that, the day after. Hush, I thought, go pee in the woods and then go back to bed, easy.

I passed the rabbits, hanging as if after a medieval execution, and the eviscerated fish. The soles of my feet were already hardening to the sticks underfoot. I went further than usual, checked repeatedly for witnesses, paused to listen for footsteps, for snapping twigs, before I pulled down my pyjamas and squatted. Flaunting yourself naked in the woods for anyone to see. You can't see the colour when you pee on the ground but there was a strong smell, I needed to drink more. No paper; I shook myself and did an inadequate job with a leaf before waddling over the warm puddle and covering myself again. The brushed cotton hurt my skin. I looked away from the rabbits as I passed again, didn't want to see the blue-white gleam of their severed spines. Mum did want them jointed, said a stew would be a whole lot easier than setting up a spit and also, she added quickly, surely more authentic, wouldn't they have wanted to stretch the meat with veg just like people today? You could see Dad wanting to see small pink bodies skewered over the flames but the Prof said yes, almost certainly, not that the middens offer much of a clue about cooking methods but common sense has its place. Fine then, Dad said, Silvie can joint them tomorrow, show the lads how it's done.

Hi Silvie.

Molly. Loo-roll in one hand, trowel in the other. Buttoned pyjamas with blue tulips on them, plaits undoing themselves in a haze of blonde. I glanced towards the hut. Shh, I whispered. Hello. I was just – I was in the wood. I know, she said, I get up early so I can poo in private, isn't it horrible, I'm amazed it's even legal. Shh, I said, yes, you're allowed to poo in the woods, people've been doing it for millennia, you just make sure you dig a hole and fill it in afterwards. Yeah, she said, and people have been dying of cholera and dysentery for centuries, yay for nature's way. Cholera was in cities, I said, it happens when sewage gets into the water supply, they'd have had more sense out here. Great, she said, they could die another day of infected hunting injuries and childbirth. Shh, I said. I'm going back in, enjoy the woods. Wait, she said, Silvie, what happened to your back, there? I pulled my pyjama top back up over my shoulder. Sunburn, I said, you've got it too. She touched my shoulder and I flinched. Not like that I haven't, she said. It's nothing, I said, it's fine, I should get back, I don't want him to – I'm still tired, should get some more sleep if I can, see you later.

I could hear him snoring from outside the door. I ducked back in and stood there waiting for my eyes to adjust, and then stepped cautiously, trailing my fingers along the splintery wall, until I could kneel on my bunk and ease myself down onto my front. This is not going to work, I thought, I can't get through today, not like this, it's too sore, it's never been this bad before, but I knew that I could and would. It was not as if there was an alternative.

The day was bright again, as if England had forgotten how to rain. The bracken is always the first to turn, bronze already coming through at midsummer, but it was still a steadfast deep green. It seemed as if all the flowers were out at once, purple and yellow vetch, foxgloves, of course the heather on the uplands. Even the harebells in the woods and honeysuckle which should have been over by now were still deliriously blooming. I kept my mind on the flora as I moved around stiffly, shoulders held back trying to stop the tunic grazing my skin, avoided sitting down until Dad told me to. You'll spill your breakfast, he said, show some respect for your mother's cooking, I won't have you wandering about like that. I dropped my gaze and did as I was told. It hurt. I'm not very hungry today, said Moll, sorry Alison.

Silvie's to joint those rabbits this morning, my dad said. Alison, you two make sure they're ready when folk are wanting them this time, hear me? In company,

75

I risked it, wanted him to know I still had a mind and a voice: yeah, but it's hard, Dad, to have the lunch on the table at one sharp for seven people who are being guided by their bellies not the clock. Mum drew her breath. So what, I thought, hit me again, I dare you, in front of all these people, let's have a public beating, an Iron-Age ritual of pain, go on, try it. Don't be thicker than you can help, Silvie, he said, that's why you have it ready in good time, so there's food when folk are wanting it. Get to work now. He met my gaze. You can sit on that rock by the rack, should be comfortable there, hm? Dan stood up. I'll do it, he said, me and Pete. We need to know how. Silvie can go with Moll, she did most of the butchering yesterday. Happen you'll need her to show you how, said Dad. I'll do that, said the Prof, keep my hand in, my wife likes her meat in cubes on plastic trays, haven't had the chance to do this for years. Go on, girls. Pick some more of those garlic greens, take the foraging book and see what else you can find, we should be getting more roots and leaves at this time of year. There was wild thyme, I said, up on the moor. Aye, said Dad, but the man said roots and leaves, didn't he, not herbs, it's not an excuse to go ramping off over the moors, you girls stay local if you've

76

no-one with you, hear me? Yes, Dad, I said. We will. Mum, I guessed, was staying home doing the washing up again, and that was her problem.

Leaving the camp with Molly felt like sneaking out of school at break to buy sweets, before I joined the sixth form and we were allowed to leave the premises so all the glamour went out of the newsagent down the road. We hurried at first, feet quick over the sun-dappled twigs and leaves as if someone might call us back. Come and dismember small mammals after all, take this down to the stream and scrub it. Molly went first, the plaits bouncing and snaking on her brown tunic. I felt my own scalp itch; I supposed there wasn't a lot of Iron-Age hair-washing. People used to use cow's urine, Dad had said with satisfaction, though he couldn't explain why. He would enjoy handing the two of us a bucket of cow piss and instructing us to put our heads in it. I stumbled over a branch, caught myself. Molly stopped. Sorry, I'm going too fast, I just somehow couldn't wait to get away. She held out her hand. You OK? I gave the hand a squeeze and let go. Her fingers were warmer than mine, dry and strong. Yeah, I said, fine, I just tripped. So where are we going, I said, should we look at the book, if there're any garlic greens left they'll be in shaded hedgerows or maybe in sunnier bits of woodland. Nah, she said, fuck that, we're going to Spar.

We set off again. The path was too narrow for us to walk side by side. But what about the foraging, I said, we can't go back there with a pack of crisps and say hey, guess what we found under a hedge. What if we buy some veg, she said, and rough them up a bit, roll them in the mud. I scampered at her heels. Won't work, you can't forage farmed veg, it's just stealing, Dad'd have a fit, they're expecting wild plants. Well then, she said, we'll find some, but after Spar, it's not as if they can say it's taken us too long or we didn't find enough, the Prof keeps saying how it's not like shopping and you can't go out with a list knowing you'll be back in time to cook to the six o'clock news, maybe today it takes a while and we don't find much. OK, I said, but we can't go back empty-handed, seriously, my dad would completely lose it. Mm, she said, does he do that often, Silvie?

Something lurched, as if I'd just gone too fast over a hill in a car. No, I said, it's fine, I mean I know he was a bit short with us yesterday but he's like that, he doesn't mean it. Yeah, she said, I'm kind of more interested in what people do and say than what they mean, I learnt that after my dad left. I could sense the approach of a story I didn't want to hear. One of my friends' mums had tried the same thing when Claire and I were passing through her kitchen on the way out: Silvie, you know Claire's Auntie Karen, my sister? Did our Claire tell you she's left her husband now? He'd been hitting her, turns out, her and the kids, a few folk'd had their suspicions. No, I'd said, Claire didn't mention that, how sad, anyway me and Claire were about to go out, if that's OK.

Molly and I were coming to the edge of the wood. Beyond the trees the sun came down hard and I found myself covering my eyes with my forearm. Hey, Molly said, it's not that bad, take a minute to get used to it. Must say, I didn't think sunburn was going to be a problem up here, actually I brought jumpers and a coat, Jim said it's always cold up north. Mm, I said. I had not understood until meeting the students that we lived 'up north', that we were 'Northerners'. Up from where? It's probably about the same as where you live, I said, you know there's the whole of Scotland further north, we're really about in the middle here. No, it's definitely colder here, she said, it does feel different. And the nights are shorter. Now if we go along this track we'll come to the road and then it's all of ten minutes to the shop, only we'll look right prats if anyone sees us. We look right prats whether anyone sees us or not, I said, and they've probably heard all about it by now anyway, round here.

Molly was right. The first car to pass slowed and two boys leant out and shouted at us, hey up love, bound for Sherwood forest are ya? Molly gave them two fingers, as if she didn't care, as if there were no possible consequences for a girl making obscene gestures on the public highway. Fuckers, she said as they drove off, hope they drive into a bridge next time. Moll! I said, though I didn't really think ill-wishing had power. What, she said, serve the bastards right. Look, there's Spar, told you. I'm going to have an ice-cream, what about you? Dunno, I said, I'll see what they've got. I'll see what I can afford, I meant; even though I was in the sixth form and there was casual work going in town, Dad had forbidden me to get a Saturday job. No need for that, you're fed and housed and there's plenty wants doing at home if you've time on your hands, you get on with your school work and then you won't have to spend your life in a shop like your mum. Either he wanted me to have a better life than his and Mum's or he knew that money is power and didn't want me to have any, or maybe – probably – both. Mum slipped me the odd couple of quid and didn't always ask for the change when she sent me to the shops.

Sweat trickled under my arms and I wiped my upper lip on the back of my hand. The shop was on the horizon where the road went up hill, and behind it a mirage of the moor wavered and floated between tarmac and sky. High above, silently, a plane left no trail. We do have to do some foraging, I said, they'll be wondering where we are. I do have to get something to eat, Molly said, something with some taste and energy in it, I reckon I'd rather live in the shadow of nuclear war with ice-cream and crisps and conditioner than in primitive purity with half-ground grains and rabbits' guts. I decided not to say anything prissy about literacy, not to mention safe water and antibiotics, and anyway she was right. Do you think someone's going to find a grassy mound in 2991, I said, and excavate it and conclude that we venerated drinking vessels and plastic packaging at the crossroads of our sacred ways? Well, she said, they'd be right, wouldn't they.

I let Molly go in first. Hung back, would have waited outside except that I reckoned I'd look even more stupid hanging about out there on my own in tunic and moccasins than trailing Molly around three aisles of highly processed and over-packaged food. She held the door for me. Come on, she said, it's fine, I've been here pretty much every day, they're used to it. She took a basket and strode around, mirrored in the black and white CCTV over her head. A bag of apples, a multi-pack of Hula Hoops, a small sack of 'fun sized' Mars bars, though why it should be more fun to have smaller chocolate bars I have never understood. A pastel box of Fondant Fancies. Dan's guilty secret, she said, his gran used to buy them and there's something about watching a hairy six-foot bloke eating pink cakes that's worth every penny.

The bell over the door rang and a woman came in, a woman wearing shapely grey linen and flat shoes like a version of our moccasins made by someone who knew how to make shoes. She looked me up and down. Good morning, she said. Red lipstick, bobbed hair with purposeful white streaks. Hi, I said. Er, good morning. Sorry. Why are you sorry, she said. I looked for Molly, who was leaning over the freezer by the till making a careful study of the ice-creams. I seemed to have forgotten how to behave in the presence of electric lights and painted walls. Don't know, I said, sorry. You must be with the archaeologists, she said. Re-enactors, whatever they're called. Yeah, I said, we're living like Iron-Age Northumbrians, I mean, obviously they didn't go to Spar and buy cake so we're not, actually, but I mean that's why we're here, in these clothes. Right, she said, and how's that going? Apart from the need for cake? Of course we heard about you, in the village, it sounds very interesting.

Erm, OK, I said, fine, we're learning a lot, well, I'm not a student, I don't have to, but I think they are. Anyway, my friend – I gestured towards Molly, who was studying a pack of Chorley cakes. I guessed they didn't have Chorley cakes in the South.

Isn't it much harder, the woman said, to find food now all the land is farmed, do you think it would have been easier for them with more wild plants and animals, greater what do you call it? Moll looked up. Biodiversity, she said. Yeah, probably. Plus they'd have known what they were doing and not been wandering round with some book with completely useless black-and-white photos to tell you which ones are poisonous. There are people in the village who'd know which ones are poisonous, said the woman, my Aunt Edith would have known, retired civil servant but she knew her plants, you could probably ask any farmer.

Molly left her basket on the freezer and came over, still holding the Chorley cakes. You mean if the Prof was into asking people who know rather than looking it all up in books, she said, yeah, I know, but it's like asking for directions, it's one thing for a bloke to admit he doesn't know something but acknowledging that someone else does know is a step too far. Moll, I said, they're not all the same, I've definitely had men ask me directions, you don't like it when Dan talks about women like that. They ask you 'cos you're not threatening, she said, and I bet there's been a five-act drama in that car first. The woman laughed. Maybe they're just socialized that way and can't help it, poor dears, she said. Maybe the drama is because they hate being like that and wish they were allowed to admit uncertainty. I'm Trudi, she said, Trudi Kelley, I'm a midwife and I live in the village, the little house just above the farm. If you ever find you need anything while you're here, advice about plants for example or a cup of tea or maybe just a hot shower, you know where I am. Enjoy your Iron-Age food.

We walked down the road, Molly eating her Cornetto and me nibbling at a lemonade ice lolly that was already melting and making my fingers sticky. Anxiety was rising in me like water in a jug. The lolly had a bitter aftertaste. I let the bit in the middle that's hard to bite without choking yourself on the stick slide onto the tarmac. Moll, I said, let's at least get off the road with all this stuff, let's just go behind the hedge and put that plastic bag away, and we must get on and find some proper food, something wild, it might take us a while. It's fine, she said, calm down, we'll finish these and then start looking, OK, we'll have more energy and it's not as if they're expecting us back at a particular time, the day's long enough. He'll know, I said, he'll know we've been mucking about, that woman might talk, please, Moll, let's just hide what you bought and do what we're supposed to be doing. He'll know, she said, licking her ice cream. Your dad. Silvie, you're terrified of him. I'm not, I said, really I'm not, but please can we just get on now, we're going to get into so much trouble. I was starting to fight my breathing, could get air out but not in, as if my body was already full up, as if there was no space inside my ribs. Hey, Moll said, sure, come on, whatever makes you feel better. Are you OK? Look, I'm putting the plastic bag in the basket, see, no-one can see if that's foraged – foraged gruel or Hula Hoops, and there, ice-cream all gone. Calm down, Silvie, it's all right.

She agreed to hide her bag of ill-gotten goods in a hedge by the wood, and we went up along the edge of the trees and the moor. We found a wild plum tree covered in early small yellow plums, sour but edible, and then a whole lot of burdock. I know you can eat the roots, I said, I'm less sure about the leaves, though I think that's what's in dandelion and burdock. In what, asked Molly. The drink, I said, you know, but she didn't know, maybe it was something else you could only get up north. Right, said Molly, but we haven't got a spade. They probably didn't have a spade in the Iron Age either, I said, we'll make do, but of course in the end I made do while Molly read bits of the foraging book out loud to me. It says here, she said, roots are probably the least practical of all wild vegetables, being labour-intensive to gather and actually in many cases illegal. You can make a burdock and rabbit stew, I said, and we can look for more garlic greens and come to think of it dandelion leaves though I don't think you'd want to cook them, best in a salad maybe with sorrel though I haven't seen any sorrel. Plenty of dandelions any road. I'm sure you *can* make a burdock and rabbit stew, said Molly, there's no law of man nor God stops you putting things in a pan if you're so minded, question is— yes, I said, well, it's exactly the kind of thing they want, isn't it, Dad and Prof Slade? She shrugged. Suppose so.

I went on grubbing at the burdock with a flat stone, feeling the soil lodging under my fingernails. The smell of damp earth rose in the heat. I switched from kneeling to squatting although both hurt the backs of my legs, tried to edge into the shade of the trees. A wind ruffled through the leaves overhead but I barely felt it on my hot face. No birds sang, no creatures scurried. The sun didn't seem to move in the sky. Slowly, I disclosed the root. Sweat trickled. The plant began to topple and I found myself feeling guiltier about killing it than I had about gutting the rabbits. The whole of life, I thought, is doing harm, we live by killing, as if there were any being of which that is not the case. Molly, I said, why did you come, if you don't like Professor Slade, if you think the whole thing's ridiculous? She bit a plum and puckered her lips. The field trip's part of the course, she said, experiential archaeology, and I took that because I liked the idea that you can learn from doing things, that it's not all books and speculation. Plus I thought it might be useful for getting into museum courses, 'cos that's about actual things too. The burdock fell. I started digging through its roots. But now you're here, I said, you're not – well, you're not exactly taking it seriously, are you? Well, she said, I'm joining in, I'm picking plums, I gathered mussels, I helped your mum wash tunics in the stream, I just think a lot of it's boys playing in the woods. Your dad and Jim, have you noticed, they're not much interested in the foraging and cooking, they just want to kill things and talk about fighting, why would I take it seriously? Because they are men, I thought, because they're in charge, because there will be consequences if you don't. I didn't see how she could not know that.

We returned to the camp to find that only Mum was there. The fire was burning, flames almost invisible in the sunlight, steam rising from the cauldron balanced on its stones. Mum sat against the wall in the shade of the hut, not apparently occupied. Maybe this was 'sitting down'. Hello, I said, look, we found burdock for your stew and more of those greens the Prof liked and loads of plums though I think ideally they'd want sugar, we can maybe dry them for sweetness. Hello, she said, hello Molly, that's good, Silvie, your dad'll be pleased. She started to get up, using her hands like a much older person. I put the rabbit on, she said, reckoned it could take a fair while, don't think those were the youngest bunnies on the hill somehow. If we get those roots scrubbed they can go in now and we'll leave the greens for later. Oh, now are you two hungry, only there's nowt ready yet. No, we said, we're fine, ate loads of plums, no bother to wait while the others get back. Could be a while, she said, warningly, as if she hadn't just told us there was nothing to eat anyway. Not but what they'll near to melt, rushing about up there, day like today. There's water on the moor, I said, springs still rising, they'll not parch, it's the sunburn I'd be thinking of. Well, she said, they're grown men the lot of them. Take these burdocks down the stream will you, give them a good wash. Molly, if you can stand the sun you could lay some of the plums to dry, it's the right weather for it an' all. Molly turned the sour plums in her basket with her fingers, picked out a caterpillar. Won't they go mouldy, she said, that's what happens to half the fruit at home. Not if they're turned, I said, you want to turn them as they go dry and wrinkled before the underside gets mould, we'll keep an eye on them. OK, she said, whatever you say, at least it's not eviscerating rabbits.

I carried the burdocks down to the stream, the handle of the basket I'd woven cutting into my hands and the weight pulling on my shoulders. I bet they'd had some kind of backpack arrangement in the Iron Age, no-one would have wanted to lug stuff around in one hand. But Dad should be pleased, it was a good haul of food.

The stream was shallower and slower than it had

been a few days earlier, but still the colour of whisky in a bottle, murmuring over the stones. I chanced it, didn't take my tunic off but rolled it up and perched gingerly on a smooth rock in the stream while I rubbed soil off the burdock roots with my hands. Cold water wavered over my legs, stroked some of the soreness from my skin. I imagined the shame carried away like blood in the water, visible first in weedy streams, curling and flickering like smoke and then dissolving, fading, until although you knew it would always be there you couldn't see it any more.

I wondered what they were doing on the moor, the men, what they'd found that was keeping them baking under the sun with the heather and the insects. There was a rounded hummock up there on a rise not far above the trees, east of the track at a point where it was and would always have been visible on a clear day for miles on the rolling tops. The map marked it 'prehistoric monument' in the Gothic font that the Ordnance Survey uses to show respect for the traces of those whose maps did not survive, and according to the Prof there was a cup and ring mark that none of the rest of us could see incised on one of the big stones. Dad would be fascinated by it as he was by the standing stones and the outlines of the hill fort above the town at home, but the Prof wasn't, so far as I could gather, that kind of archaeologist and he'd already explained to Dad that he wasn't funded or equipped to dig this summer. That's not what we're here for, he'd said, I hope that was clear when we arranged for you to join us, I might get a paper out of this but it's teaching, mostly, little more than a game. Aye, said Dad, I knew that, right enough, course I did.

The burdocks were clarted with clayey soil and even once I'd got the lumps off I had to rub every root with my fingertips. I flexed my feet, stroked the green waterweed growing over a stone with my toes. Slimy and soft. Dad would like to find a body up there, I thought, most of all he would like to be the one out gathering peat to see us through the winter, the one who, aching after hours of honest labour, leans on the spade once again, levers the clod that's lain for centuries over the compacted prehistoric trees of the peat bog and sees among the roots and frantic worms a human face, a face last seen two thousand years ago by the neighbours who led their friend naked across the moor, who bound him hand and foot.

I piled pale clean roots on my lap, felt the wet tunic sag between my thighs, leant down to rub my fingers in the water and watch grains of soil loosen and flow over the whorls of my skin. Dad had told me on one of our winter walks that if they gagged and blindfolded the bog people, it wasn't so's the victims couldn't see what was coming, they knew fine well what was coming and it didn't matter what kind of noise they made. No, the blindfolding and gagging were to protect the people whose job was the killing from the last looks and the curses. Makes a kind of sense, doesn't it, he'd said, if folk believe in any of that stuff, ill-wishing and cursing and what have you. You wouldn't want to hear owt they might say at the end, wouldn't want it in your ears, so to speak. But didn't the victims agree, I said, to be killed, I thought that was the idea, they ate the last meal and maybe had a few months of luxury and they suffered for it. He shrugged. We'd gone up onto the tops after Sunday lunch as usual and we were coming down the track back into town, just crossing the snow-line; behind us the sky fell darker than the gleaming moor. Happen no-one really knows, he said, some says one and some another. They don't often find defensive wounds, but then with the drugs they'd had and the way they were tied up you wouldn't necessarily expect it, happen they couldn't have put up much fight anyroad. Did something new come out, I'd asked him, did one of your professor friends send you something? Over the years, Dad had established some kind of trade in knowledge with a couple of archaeologists, men, he said, who'd passed the eleven-plus and made summat of themselves, had begun to exchange his self-taught expertise in outdoor survival, foraging and mountaincraft for their answers to his questions and offprints of their research. We'd learnt to lie low, Mum and I, when these fat letters with university stamps on them crackled through the letter box. Mostly it meant a buoyant evening, silent but for the purr of the gas fire in the sitting room and the rustle of pages as Dad read and re-read his new treasure, told us new facts about British prehistory, but sometimes something upset him, maybe the thought of those other men who were paid to walk the places Dad loved and write the ideas he could have had. Then tea was late or over-salted or Mum should have remembered he couldn't abide something he'd eaten happily enough the previous week or the least he'd hope given how little she had to do was that she'd keep a clean house. I was giving him cheek or suggesting that he and Mum weren't good enough for me or wasting something he paid for, food or water or electricity. Then things got bad. He can't help it, she'd say later, he always had a temper on him and of course he gets het up, stuck behind the wheel all day, a man like that, wanting to be outdoors, he weren't meant for it and it's a crying shame.

There were footsteps over the twigs in the wood and I scrambled off my rock, tugged at my tunic, slipped on weed, splashed, fell and dropped the clean burdocks back in the stream. My knees hurt. I stood up slowly, the tunic wet from the waist down, and there was indeed a little blood running down my leg. I wanted to cry at the shock, the indignity. I started to pick up the burdocks. Hey, said Molly, we were wondering if you'd fallen in, your mum says if we don't get t'burdocks int' pan soon they'll be hard as little green apples happen lads come home. Don't, I said, don't laugh at her like that, that's just how we speak. She sat down on the bank beside me, slipped off her shoes and put her feet in the water. I looked away. No, she said, I'm sorry, I wasn't laughing, I just love it, the phrases, I've never really heard it before, only on TV. Yeah well, I said, we're not stupid, just 'cos we don't sound like you. I know, she said, sorry, Silvie, I shouldn't have imitated her, I just really like the way it sounds. Well it's not the way you sound, I said, so don't. She touched my shoulder and I flinched. Sorry, she said again. Really

94

Silvie, don't be cross. It's OK, I said, just don't laugh at people's accents, you do know yours sounds weird to me, posh. I just really like the way it sounds, I parroted, squeaky and clipped. It's not a different country, the north of England, it's not that far from you, we're a tiny country to start off with, have you ever actually been past Birmingham before? Nope, she said, not even as far as Birmingham, actually, but I'm here now, aren't I, and I do like it, the moors and the beach, I want to get my mum up here, she'd love it. Yeah, I said, well, tell her the natives can be unpredictable and don't take kindly to mockery. I had never been as far south as Birmingham myself but I saw no particular reason to share that fact. It's just traffic and throngs of people, Dad said, down south, everything built over, no sense in going there. So do you forgive me, she said, and I, having never, so far as I knew, been asked that question by anyone before, looked at her all rosy and fair, smelling somehow of nice soap, said yeah, sure, course I do, it's fine.

The men came back late and a little excited, het up. We heard their voices coming through the trees before we heard their feet; bloody hell, said Molly, do you think women have always been hearing the approach of men from two miles off, do you think it was like the football and they could tell from the calls in the woods if the woolly mammoths or the hunters had won? I didn't like it when she talked like that, wanted to go on believing that men were also people, that there are not, in fact, two kinds of human. Women get excited too, I said, they get all shrill in groups, you can hear them laughing on trains sometimes. Mum, have they really been up there all day, without food? She'd been sitting with us under the trees, away from the heat of the dying fire, but now she got onto her hands and knees and pushed herself back to standing. Dad's right, she really should do some exercise, I thought, go back to swimming or that keep fit class, though Dad hadn't liked her doing either. Good thing we stewed them an' all, said Mum, they'd be leather by now, else. She poked in the cauldron and a surprisingly appetizing smell drifted through the summer afternoon. Bring us the greens, Silvie, should be just done when the lads've had a wash and sat down.

It turned out that Pete had fallen, up on the moor. They'd been crossing one of the bogs that should be mostly dry at this time of year and he'd misjudged a tussock and gone headlong into the mire. It sounds funny, he said, still dusted with dry bog, but it wasn't, it really does suck you in. Aye, said Dad, it does that, Silvie went in a few years back, didn't you, and we got her out fine enough but the bog kept her boot, remember now? I did. A spring day, raw and damp, snow and ice newly thawed and even through the heather the ground dull under foot. We'd had to pick our way along the beginning of the track where the dog walkers go, and up on the tops grey sky lay heavy on land in winter's dark colours. We weren't hurrying exactly, but the afternoon was wearing on, the days still short, and the mud had made for slow going on the way out and would be no better going down. There's a place up there, two ridges over from the hill fort, where the path goes straight across the marsh, which is fine in summer, treacherous in winter when only the spikes of dead reed sticking through the snow tell you where to put your feet, and mostly just a pain in the backside in between. You have to pick your way from tussock to tussock, checking for the footprints of earlier walkers and balancing on one leg to poke the ground with the other foot before you trust it. I had not been careful enough, had slipped, teetered, known one of those moments of inevitability, splashed. Cold water clutched me, earth pulled and sucked. It wasn't quicksand, I wasn't being pulled down, but I couldn't get up either and the instinctive struggle made it worse. Don't move now, girl, Dad had said, I'll get you out, don't fret, but don't you go wriggling, you're fine there, it's just water, won't go further nor skin, and he'd heaved a stone and a bleached white branch from some long-ago tree and balanced himself on them while he knelt in the mire and got his hands on my middle. I'd been sitting not waist-deep, but even so I couldn't help myself and it took him a long time to work me free. It hurt. The bog seals around you, and it will of course go further than skin, or at least will fill the inner skins of every orifice, seeping and trickling through the curls of your ears, rising like a tide in your lungs, creeping cold into your vagina, it will embalm you from the inside out. The boot it took had been firmly laced over my ankle; I couldn't have taken it off without undoing the laces but somehow the bog managed it in the struggle without me even noticing. Dad had held me when I stood again on the heather, looked away while I took off my jeans and put on the waterproof trousers he'd been carrying for me in his backpack, made me drink the last of the tea in the thermos flask. You'll maybe be best without that other boot too, lass, hard when one foot doesn't know what the other's about and we'll be heading right back, we'll get you off the moor now. He took my hand, then, most of the way down, steered me around thorns and even cowpats.

Pete's bog was smaller than the one I'd fallen in and, in August, as dry as it would ever be, but even so it had taken them a while to get him out and they'd made a mess of themselves. And we found summat, said Dad, thought for a minute we were onto – well, anyroad, it's given us an idea, summat we can try. He and the Prof exchanged glances. Pete, if you give me that smock, Mum said, that tunic, whatever you want to call it, I'll get it washed for you again. Can't say it'll be dry by morning, mind. Pete stood there. He was dry now, of course, but the rough cloth was swollen and stiff with fragments of ancient flora and water brown as bloodstains, and earth was thick under his fingernails. Defensive injuries, I thought. OK, he said, thanks Alison, if you're sure you don't mind. Pete, said Molly. What, he said. She should mind, Moll said, even if she doesn't, you should, you don't need some woman to wash your clothes for you, do it yourself. Oh, said Mum, I don't mind, it's no bother, not as if there's ironing or any of that. Dan looked from Mum to Molly, as if following a ball. Please don't do it, he's perfectly capable, said Molly. Dad looked up. Wash the lad's tunic, Alison, I've some kecks you can take while you're about it. But give us dinner first, we're all clemmed.

Mum started dishing up. Dining forks were introduced to these isles a mere five hundred years ago, give or take, but we'd convinced the Prof if not Dad that there wasn't a good reason to be sure our imaginary Iron Age diners wouldn't have used flat wooden spoons rather than fingers for stew. The Prof had agreed that we were too many to gather around the pot in the apparently authentic fashion and allowed individual bowls. Sit down, Silvie, said Dad, and I held his gaze while I took a deep breath and sat on my usual stone. It hurt. I saw his smile. Moll was watching us. So what was it you found, I said, the thing that might have been something? Oh, said the Prof, it's not that interesting, Victorian at the oldest, but it might have given us an idea or two, wouldn't you say, Bill? Aye, said Dad, happen it might. An old boot, said Dan, you're clearly not the first, Silvie, to leave a shoe in a bog. A girl's boot. How old, said Molly, can I see it? Nineteenth century, I'd say, said the Prof, and later, let me eat first, it was hungry work up there. That, I thought, was not work, that was play, that is what my dad is paying to do with all of his holiday entitlement

100

this year. You'll like it, Moll, the boot, said Pete, it's got little buttons all the way up. Not to mention a heel, said Dad, right daft thing to wear on a moor an' all, she got no less than she deserved, that one. That girl, I thought, that Victorian girl who owned a button-hook and a pair of pretty boots, where is she now, did she deserve only to lose her shoe or is she herself still there, her coiled hair reddening in the wet, her knitted shawl and lace-edged petticoat long since dissolved into the bog while the whorls on her fingers and the down on her legs toughen and outlast us all, is she curled up in the peat with the dark water in her lungs and earth stopping her mouth, hands flung out in the final struggle or folded in defeat?

I spat a shell of gristle, maybe a component of a leg joint, into my hand. Dad and I find ash, I said, up on the moor tops at home, people say they want to be scattered there as if scattering is making something go away entirely and then we sit down with our sandwiches and realise we're in the middle of someone's granny, of course they always choose the places you'd stop for lunch, somewhere on the top of a ridge with a nice view. They were all looking at me, the students. Dad was smiling. What, I said, what is it? Nothing, said Molly, never mind. Anyroad, said Dad, when it's my turn, the lass is right, I don't give a monkey's where you chuck the ashes, only don't go making a mess on the fells, you hear me Silvie? OK, I said, fine. I will dig a hole in the woods with the camping trowel, I thought, and fill it in when I'm done. Er, Professor – Jim, I said, I'd like to see the boot too, please, if you don't mind. Of course, he said. I'll be taking it into town tomorrow morning, see if the police have any interest and if not I'll send it to the department, we can at least find out exactly how old it is. I was going to pick up a couple of things anyway. For a special project. He spat out a small bone. This stew is very good by the way Alison, thank you, and what are the tubers? Roots, not tubers, I said, burdock, Molly and I found them, there's plenty more if you want them. Please, he said, they're delicious, which they were not. Molly was picking out the greens and roots and leaving her meat. What would you sacrifice to the bog, she said, what would the modern thing be, if you were really scared or really desperate for something? Mum was eating, not bothering, assuming as usual that none of this talk was meant for her, but everyone else paused, winced, which must have been how it was when men picked up their special inlaid swords, their most beautiful amulets and broke them on purpose and gave them to the still waters of bog and grove. In Denmark they found braids of human hair very much like Molly's cast into the bog, because you give what you most want to keep. You would have been able to see your votive objects, Dad had told me, for months or maybe years, and there were special walkways and platforms built out over pools and marshes perhaps partly for the purpose of visiting the murdered things. People too, this particular book suggested; they weren't necessarily gone when they were put into the bog but would have lain there, dead and still present, not going, faces wavering through the clear water, mouth and skin and hair arrested in the retreating moment of loss while time continued to pass for the rest of the community. My answer was probably honestly still Owl, not because at seventeen I was unusually attached to a stuffed toy but because I had no other particular material affections, because I had so little that I wanted.

Dan shook his head. Don't know. My guitar, maybe. You're crap at your guitar, said Pete. Yeah, but as long as I've got it I might get better, see? Anyway it was a big birthday present. What about you? Pete shrugged, but you could see there was something, something so precious he didn't want to speak of breaking it. My father's paintings, said the Prof, baby pictures of my kids. Old photos of my parents, before I was born. Right, said Molly, ancestors, progeny, the bodies of your tribe. Yes, he said, maybe, something like that. I felt Dad's gaze on me and knew with a shiver what he was thinking. My daughter. Break her and stake her to the bog, stop her before she gets away. They weren't dead, the bog people, not to those who'd killed them. They had to be pinned to their graves with sharp sticks driven through elbow and knee, trapped behind woven wooden palings, to stop them coming back, creeping home dead and not dead in the dark. A bird trilled from the bush behind me. I got up. Anyone else need more water, I said, you must have got parched up there.

The Prof had gone by the time I got up the next morning. He reappeared whistling while Molly and I were pushing rye gruel around wooden bowls that still held the flavour of last night's stew. He was wearing jeans and an ironed checked shirt with a plaited leather belt, and had the air of having had a haircut. *Spruce*, I thought, almost *dapper*, and I wondered if he used that intricate belt on his daughters, on Charlotte and Lucy, when they made him angry. Bet he went off to a hotel and had bacon and eggs for breakfast, murmured Molly, bet he had a long hot shower and sat over his coffee with the newspaper. Well, I said, he could hardly go off to the police station in a handwoven tunic, could he, and he wasn't going to take a bowl of rabbit and burdock stew for his breakfast. Anyway, we had ice-creams and you bought a whole bag of stuff, what happened to that? I still haven't had a shower, she said, not for days. What had she expected, I wondered, from Experiential Archaeology? I wasn't taking the course and I'd known it was going to be another holiday without plumbing or a proper cup of tea. All done, said the Prof, and Bill, I got those supplies we were talking about, I'll show you later.

Mum stayed at the camp again. Would you like to come too, Molly asked her, just for the walk, but she said no, she'd things to do, though I couldn't really see what things; in our version of Iron Age life the housework was pretty minimal and there wouldn't be much to cook until we got back. Leave her be, I thought, she was a grown-up, wasn't she, could have joined any of us, or gone off on her own to the beach or to Spar or even on the bus into Morbury if she'd been inclined. It was cooler that day, with hills of white cloud banking blue sky, and Dan and

Molly and I set off briskly. Pete went with Dad and the Prof on some mission of violence against the local fauna, not that the rabbit stew had not been very welcome.

We dug more burdocks, and then went up onto the moor for bilberries, which was of course the wrong way round, like shopping for ten pounds of potatoes before you go all the way across town to the post office. We could just leave them under a hedge, I said, to pick up on the way back, it's hardly likely anyone's going to nick our burdock roots, especially with the stuff free for the taking all over the place. I suppose that's what those caches were for, said Dan, the little stone mounds, not so much long-term storage as somewhere to leave your potatoes while you go to the post office. But we weren't sure which way we'd be coming back or where we'd find bilberries or, in the absence of a prehistoric cist, how we'd remember which hedge we'd used, so the burdocks came too, dragging on our arms. We didn't go to Spar, but apart from that the day felt like a repetition of the one before, the rhythms of finding and gathering, walking and squatting, talking and scattering. I found that my fingers knew how to pick the ripe berries without my mind needing to think about it, that I had learnt to see what was under the leaves or shaded by heather without consciously searching. I indulged myself with the idea that ancient knowledge runs somehow in our blood, that in time I could forget who fought in the War of the Spanish Succession and how to solve simultaneous equations, and remember how to spin yarn and grind grain, to read the flight of birds and the growth of plants to tell me what was happening beyond my sight. My father's skills: redundant except for archaeological purposes.

But when we got back, they were not busy about subsistence, nor communing with the natural world. Mum was hanging over her cauldron again and the guys were playing with big sticks, too long for firewood, and willow withies which they must have got from one of the three big trees in the field below. The sheep took refuge under them on hot days. Jesus, said Molly, they've actually made themselves Lego, haven't they, I suppose it's better than cowboys and Indians. Allies and Huns, I said, was the version we played at my primary school, I've sometimes wondered about that, if all the five-year-olds in England were still playing at bombing Germany in the late '70s or if other towns had moved on. The boys used to run around the playground with their arms wide, making bomb noises. Yeah, she said, we did that too, it is weird, do you think American kids had moved on to Vietnam? No, I said, from what I gather they mostly have real artillery and just shoot each other properly. Anyway, it won't be Lego, it's probably some kind of war-game. Iron Age cowboys and Indians.

I was only bloody right. We're seeing if we can make a ghost wall, said the Prof, sitting back on his haunches. I was just telling your dad, it's what one of the local tribes tried as a last-ditch defence against the Romans, they made a palisade and brought out their ancestral skulls and arrayed them along the top, dead faces gazing down, it was their strongest magic. Wait, said Molly, ancestral skulls? He put down his willow twigs. You know about this, Molly, we did it last term, I must say I thought it would be memorable. Two lectures, third week? Fragmented Bodies and Using Your Heads? I remember, said Pete, who was plaiting fronds of willow in a way that looked even less useful than what anyone else was doing. Good man, said the Prof. Anyway Molly, some tribes seem to have decapitated their dead and preserved the heads, in some cases for centuries, and had them on display indoors, somewhere where there were fires, maybe in the rafters of their houses. You can tell from the accumulation of soot and smoke. And Tacitus passes on a story about the skulls being used in battle somewhere around here, up by the Wall. Did the Romans notice, asked Moll, I shouldn't have thought they'd be put off by some old bones. The Prof leant forward again. He was interlacing willow to make some kind of fence-panel. Well, obviously they noticed enough for the story to get passed to Tacitus, but no, you're right, it doesn't seem to have bothered them. They approached in testudo formation, he said, you know, the tortoise effect under the wall of shields, and probably barely even saw the skulls. But it's a powerful idea, isn't it, and it speaks to the importance of human remains to the culture. Yeah, said Molly, erm, did you get anything to eat, any meat or fish? Dad looked up. Thought you'd gone vegetarian, any road.

Their failure to hunt did not seem to me the most obvious problem with the plan. Dad, I said, er, Professor Slade, what are you going to do for human remains? For your fence? Oh, said Mum, I'm boiling up the rabbits' heads. And Professor Slade stopped at the meat market, there's a couple of sheep's skulls and a cow's, not to mention skin for the drums. Dan snorted and then coughed and snorted again. What, he said, ghost rabbits, you serious? With their little teeth? He made a rabbit face and Molly giggled. Tortoise formation, she said, wonder who'll get there first. That's a hare, dumbo, said Dan. I could see Dad's face darken. Don't, I thought, don't laugh at him, it won't be you who catches it, don't make him feel stupid. Yes, well, said the Prof, the university does have an Ethics Committee, not sure I'd get away with using undergraduates for the purpose though you never know, maybe we could do it to people who cheat in exams. What did you bring us, Molly? More delicious burdock, she said, I hear it's especially good with rabbits' brains, and bilberries for those of more delicate disposition, by which I mean me. Dad muttered. You'll eat what you're given, girl. I beg your pardon, Mr Hampton, said Molly, I didn't catch that. My stomach clenched. Stop it, you don't know what you're stirring up, you have no idea how this goes, you can't speak to him like that. I said, Dad said, looking up, enunciating clearly, I said picky lasses went hungry, back then, I said it weren't for the likes of you to say who gets what. Ah, um, said the Prof, well, as I said I don't know that we can really reflect the gender hierarchies of prehistory here, inasmuch as we know what they might have been, I'm sure Molly meant no harm, plenty of berries to go round, aren't there, Moll and Silvie do you want to – to go – well, why don't you go see if you can find a little more of that wild thyme, hmm, I'm afraid we've rather distracted Alison, may be a while before there's cooked food so you two just have a little potter up the stream, hm, see what you come by?

Dad looked at him a moment, at me, and went back to weaving his ghost fence. I could feel already my skin shrinking and tightening, the hand across my face, the belt on my legs, the shame, and I saw Mum's hands shake as she stirred the bones in the pan. Rabbit magic, said Dan, shaking his head, and I flinched.

I found some cress. I thought it might placate Dad. Molly sat on a stone and trailed her feet in the water, though it wasn't really hot enough for that to seem much fun. Her toenails were painted sparkly gold now, and you could see the outline of her moccasins in the suntan on her feet. Any more of that business, she said, and I'm off to Morbury on the bus for a pie and chips, he's a right chauvinist pig, he seems to think we all have to do what he says, he's not the professor here. She leant forward to pick a quartz pebble from the bed of the stream and one of her plaits dipped into the water. He's just taking it seriously, I said, he drives buses all year, he's not like the Prof, this is his one chance to do what he's really interested in. What about your mum, said Molly, when does she get to do what she's interested in? I shrugged and went on nipping off stalks of cress with my fingernails. Obviously Mum was not interested in things, never had been, you only had to look at her to see that. Does he ever even ask her what she thinks, Moll went on. Why, I said, what about your mum, what does she do, what is she interested in. If you've got all the answers, I didn't say, if you know how people ought to live. I ate a leaf of cress, more peppery than I was expecting. My eyes watered. She's a teacher, said Moll, she teaches Physics, and yes she has interests, she does stuff. Aerobics. Gardening, she grows vegetables. Weird ones, mostly, says there's no point growing stuff you can buy at the supermarket though some of us might think there are reasons the shops don't stock what she grows. She'd like your cress. I'll tell her about the burdocks. Keep fit and gardening, I thought, down south, in Hertfordshire wherever that is, bet they've got a huge house and garden, bet it's the first time she's sat down to eat with a bus driver and a supermarket cashier. She squeezed water out of the paintbrush-end of her plait. My dad left us, she said, when I was five. Mum's coped on her own since then, he doesn't even pay anything. She looked up. I'm proud of her. Yeah, I said, she sounds great. She didn't understand, I thought, she couldn't see what it was like for us. Try some of the cress, I said.

The guys were more interested in building the Ghost Wall, the Rabbit Palisade, than in eating, even once Mum had done her best with a sort of thyme dumpling. Molly stood with her arms folded, watching Dad and the Prof and now Dan and Pete weaving the willow lattice and trying to fasten the drumskins tight to their willow hoops. The wall was going to be big, and unless Molly and I went out foraging again, there was not going to be much by way of dinner. Mum had fished the rabbits' skulls out of the cooking pot and lined them up in the sun to dry, like the heads of Tudor criminals. Memento mori. Poor bloody rabbits. The Prof had got the other skulls out of his car and they gazed eyeless from the rock where Mum often sat, their whiteness still shiny and tinged with blue, indecently exposed not weathered. The human skulls, I supposed, the ghost skulls, would have been leaf-brown, polished by long handling and by the smoke of decades of cooking fires, artefacts as much as body parts. I don't know whether to laugh or cry, said

Molly, it kind of reminds me of Swallows and Amazons but they're grown men. Those little drums and a willow fence with rabbits' heads on top, for what, to keep out the Romans? I'm off, she said, Jim, I'll be back later. Oh, said the Prof, yes, OK. Dad knelt up and watched as she walked off, shook his head. Spoilt little bitch. Silvie, go help your mum, she's the dinner to get yet.

THEY SET UP the ghost wall towards sunset. The shadows of trees and grass leant long through air hazy with slanting gold light. Molly hadn't come back and I was beginning to worry; I couldn't think what she could find to do for all this time, or how she would get back after dark. Mum saw us beginning to carry the panels up the hill and said she was going to bed, but I hung around, wanting to see what happened, not wanting to spend longer than I had to in the dark hut. It was getting colder and Mum came back out with the blanket from my bed and folded it around my shoulders. There, she said, no need to go catching your death of cold, I'm sure they had the sense to keep warm, back in the day, what about your feet. I'm fine, Mum, I said, thanks, you get some rest. Well, she said, don't stay up all night.

Silvie, bring the skulls now, said Dad.

I approached the cow's head, its white bright against the softening colours of stones and grass. There were still shreds of dried flesh around the eye-sockets and it still, more or less, had ears. I didn't want to touch it, felt as if I should do some reverence, ward off something, before picking it up. Its teeth grinned. I reached out and touched it between the eye-sockets. It wasn't cold, nor quite dry. I would need to carry it in both hands, under the jaw. I would need to hold it tight against me. Silvie, called Dad, did you hear me, I said bring the skulls. I turned to the line of rabbits, to the sheep's heads, more familiar from the dry bones encountered sometimes at the feet of crags and the edges of mountain streams. When I was little Dad had to lead me past them with my eyes closed, holding my hand. It's just bones, Silvie, we all have them, you wouldn't be out here walking, else. I didn't then like the thought of my own bones, waiting inside me for their own eventual exposure. I went round behind the stone and picked up the cow's skull, carried it facing forwards up the dimming hill.

Even Dan seemed to be working seriously now, quietly as the sun slipped towards the western moorland. Shadows reached. The noise of the day, the birds and small rustlers, the wind in the leaves, even perhaps the distant wash of traffic on the Great North Road, stilled. The moon, waxing, a couple of days off full, was crossing the eastern horizon, beginning to stand out from the deepening sky. I stood there, my hands cupping the space of whatever bovine desire and fear had been within that skull. I watched the men hammer posts and fix their woven panels. Mad play, the building of a wall where there was nothing inside, the conjuring of animal spirits on a summer's night.

Bring the other bones, Silvie, don't just stand about, it'll be dark before we know it.

I brought the small heads one at a time in hands cupped as if to receive the body of Christ, the blood and bones of my fingers and palms a final brief protection. There had been minds there. Sheep cry for their taken lambs, even rabbits know alarm and need. I raised each one as a sacrament to the ghost wall, found myself bowing my head as Dad set them in place.

They made drumming, as the eastern sky darkened and stars prickled above the band of pale cloud. They made chanting, and I found myself joining in, heard my voice rise clear, hold its notes, above their low incantation. We sat on the ground before our raised bone-faces, sang to them as they gleamed moonlit into the darkness. We sang of death, and it felt true. Away to the south, orange light spilled across the sky from the town, and below us a single pair of headlights nosed the lane.

Why not, after all, make ceremony for the animal dead, for those we have deliberately killed. There is still a dying.

WE SLEPT LATE, all except Mum, who had a breakfast of bilberries and griddle-cakes ready before I came out of the hut, still in my pyjamas, to find the sun sharp in my eyes and the tree-shade already contracted. You were up late, she said, or I daresay early, sun must've been up again time you and him come in. Yeah, I said, nearly, I'm just off to the wood. I wandered through the trees until I found the bush that had become my peeing place, a very un-Iron-Age rhododendron under whose spreading skirts I could pull down my pyjamas and squat in reasonable security. I stroked the backs of my thighs, which were still sore, and when I stood up craned and lifted my top to see that the marks on my back were less angry. In a few days it would be over, until next time. And Molly, I remembered, had she come back? I should have thought of her last night,

119

should not have been so absorbed that I forgot her altogether.

Of course she came back, said Mum, I waited up, how did you not see the car? Some lad brought her, bit the worse for wear if you ask me, the both of them, shouldn't have been behind the wheel, I'd say. Don't tell your dad. Not surprised if she's still sleeping it off. Don't tell your dad now mind. He's off to the stream for a wash, get yourself dressed before he's back. You know I wouldn't tell him, I said, I'm not daft.

I thought there might be embarrassment on the air, an awkwardness at the memory of the Prof drumming with his head thrown back to the moon, at Dad himself sitting straight as if in church and joining a wordless chant, the two sceptical boys in the end not exchanging glances but intent on the bone-faces on high and swaying to rough music. I was wrong. Mum and I gave each other one look as Dad and the Prof stepped in and did a strange male back-slapping move, like gorillas. I had never seen Dad touch another man before, didn't know he knew the steps. Great evening, said the Prof, amazing, what we did there. Yeah, said Dad, late night though, we've missed the best of the day. It happens, said the Prof, I'm sure it happened back then, the long summer nights, plenty of dark for sleeping in the winter. The breakfast's all ready, said Mum, I can make you some tea if you want it, leastways herbal.

Molly and I went off foraging again. I don't think it was even discussed: Mum was doing whatever Mum did, the boys were going with Dad and the Prof and whatever they were doing was important and didn't need to be shared with the rest of us, Molly and I were dealing with plants, which required no ceremony. I've got food, said Molly, don't worry, I stocked up in town yesterday, so we can go dig up more weird roots or whatever but first I want you to show me this ghost wall. It's still there, right? This way? She set off through the trees and I followed her. Far's I know, I said. I didn't want her to see, knew it was going to look stupid under morning light. It was just a game, I said, just to see how things might have been, obviously it's not a real ghost wall. Mm, she said, a real ghost wall, shall we think about that? I could see it now, below the brow of the hill, a rickety palisade and the cow's skull balanced against the blue sky. Of course I know it's not real, I said, but none of this is real, is it, this whole summer, the blankets came from a shop and you lot made the moccasins on a study day and the Prof had the grains delivered from the health food shop in

Morbury, that's not the point. So what is the— she said. How was your evening, I said, you got a lift back? She grinned. Yes I did. Well, with a bit of an interlude in a car park on the way, and very nice too. And I'm getting a lift back in again tomorrow. Come too, if you like, he's got friends. Come where, I thought, a pub in Morbury, to drink and talk to men? Can't, I said, no way Dad would let me. It's there, look. The ghost wall.

Molly went up to the fence, stroked its weave. Her plaits, I saw, were woven too, their rhythm echoing the work of my dad's hands. That's seriously weird, she said, the heads. I thought it was just a bit naff but that's creepy, they're like trophies or something. What did you do last night, dance around them? No, I said, there was no dancing. Where do you want to go this morning, I asked, there's not much on the moor except the bilberries, we could maybe go back to the beach, it's not so hot and the tide's out mid-afternoon. But damn, I thought, she will want to swim, she'll think we should take our clothes off and she would see my back. Or we can try that next wood, I said, it's too early for blackberries still but there might be more plums and maybe mushrooms, Dad could tell us if we picked anything poisonous. Molly was gazing at the sheep's skulls, hands behind her back as if she might be tempted and didn't want to touch them. Don't mind, she said. Woods. It's too far to the beach. You sure your dad knows his mushrooms? Yes, I said, I'm sure. We turned away, began to walk back down the hill towards our foraging places. Silvie, she said, you're really OK with this, the ghost wall? It's interesting, I said, I didn't think it would be but it is. You're not scared, she said. I shrugged. Of what, bones? Of people, she said. Of your dad and Jim. Nah, I said, why would I be scared, we just said it's not real.

We set off back to the woods, not hurrying. Molly said she'd been yesterday to visit the midwife, Trudi. But you can't just go to someone's house like that, I said, we only met her once. Well she did invite us, Molly said, she said if we wanted a hot shower we could go there and I did want a hot shower, I couldn't go out with my hair all greasy, so I went and she was in. You should go too. Trudi had given her tea, with home-made cake that was a present from the mother of a patient, and let Molly use her expensive shampoo; I don't think it surprised either of us that the brands Molly found exciting meant nothing to me. It felt so good, Molly said, a proper shower, I feel so much better, and she says we can go back any time.

She's really interested in what we're doing here, she likes the Roman stuff. We could probably go tomorrow, if you like. No, I said, it would feel weird, I'll get Mum to heat some water for my hair, or I can just use the stream, that's what I do when we're camping in Scotland. We found another plum tree and I climbed it and shook the branches while Molly skipped around gathering falling fruit. They did eat a lot of fruit and veg, I said, must have been such a relief when someone invented bread. And ovens. And pies. Come down and have some biscuits, said Molly, here, I bought them yesterday. Bet no-one got fat, anyway, she said, and poked her own belly as if she thought there was something wrong with it. I don't know, I said, they had time to make jewellery, didn't they, and to have rituals and festivals and decorative objects, they weren't all busy with subsistence the whole time, there must have been a surplus at least sometimes. Yeah, said Molly, that or the women spent all their time foraging and cooking so the men could play with Lego and bang drums and howl at the moon. I did hear you, you know, when I got back, your mum and I had a bit of a giggle. I ate another biscuit. It was weird, I said, the way it went from being a bit daft to feeling like something real. I didn't know people could decide to make that happen. Have some peanuts, she said, lots of energy and protein, what do you mean decide to make that happen? I shrugged. Don't know. Like in a church, I suppose, do something that would be really silly if you did it in the street or even on your own in a room, but somehow it's not when everyone joins in. Silvie, she said, you're scaring me, this is sounding like a cult. What, I said, Dad and the Prof and some rabbits? Let's see if we can find those mushrooms, I saw some in the wood the other day. Yes, she said, Silvie, what happened to your legs? I could see them, you know, when you were up the tree. The marks.

Oh. My heart flopped under my breastbone, as if I'd been caught out. A teacher had noticed once, changing for PE, but it wasn't illegal for a parent to use reasonable chastisement and there were still plenty of teachers in post who had wielded canes and rulers in their day. Children's bodies were not their own, we were all used to uncles who liked to cop a feel given half a chance and mums who showed love in smacked legs. I cheeked my dad, Miss, got a walloping. Yes well, she said, I can't say I'm entirely surprised.

Nothing, I said, must have been a trick of the light. She looked at me. I looked away. He hits you, she said, your dad. He's been hitting you here. You're scared of him. No, I said, no I'm not, of course I'm not, you don't know what you're talking about, maybe— I stopped. Maybe you're jealous because your dad left you, because he doesn't love you, because he doesn't care enough to teach you a lesson. Haven't you been listening, people don't bother to hurt what they don't love. To sacrifice it. It's nothing, Moll, I said, really, there's nothing wrong. OK, she said, fine, you don't have to talk about it. But there is something wrong. It's not OK for someone to hit you.

THE NEXT DAY was the hottest we'd had, shimmering and windless. By mid-morning you could smell the heather baking underfoot on the moor, and the telephone mast on the horizon floated and wavered as if it had gone adrift. When I went into the woods the shade under the oak trees felt cavernous but there was no memory of cool ground even in the middle of the forest; the air fizzed with midges that massed on exposed skin as soon as I stopped moving. I felt as if I could still hear the beat of the night-time drums, as if somewhere in my head or my guts they went on sounding. After breakfast Dad and the Prof went off up the hill to the moor again, as though they were negotiating the end of the Cold War up there rather than playing at Picts and Romans. We're working on an idea, said the Prof, we might have something rather special to do later. Foraging again, you lot, you might go back to the beach, the mussels are an obvious protein source. Pete and Molly looked at each other, visibly remembering the heat of our last beach trip. The tide's just coming up at the moment, said Dan, I suppose we could go later this afternoon, it should be cooler then as well. There'll be hazels by now, Dad said, if you know where to look, keep better and safer than mussels an' all. Hazelnuts, said Dan, really, they grow wild? Yes, I said, and you can eat them green, if you've ever had cobnuts they're just a cultivated version. Oh, OK, he said, thanks, and I blushed. Little Miss Show-Off.

I couldn't really remember where hazels were likely to grow, and anyway no-one else much cared. The others were tired, it was clear that the grown-ups' attention was not on us, they wanted to sit somewhere shady and chat about people and plans that they knew and I didn't. I'd never seen Dad as distracted from me and Mum as he was then but I didn't trust that he'd forget what he'd told me to do. The hazels were just a suggestion, Sil, said Dan, he didn't say you had to. I didn't tell him that Dad didn't make suggestions, but after a while I left them sitting at the top of the woods batting at midges and arguing about who'd got most drunk the previous term. I wandered through the trees, heading vaguely down hill although there wasn't a path, treading quietly for no particular reason. Pete's voice and Molly's laughter came winding through the branches for some time after I'd stopped hearing Dan. The drums beat in my head. Skin drums, sheepskin, and when I listened I heard a sheep call from the hillside. They hear the drums too, I thought, the sheep and the rabbits, the owls and foxes, they pass by and see the skulls raised high, their own skulls. I licked sweat off my upper lip and let the twigs scratch my arms as I pushed past. I was hungry again.

I found a hazelnut tree in the end, but then I couldn't find the students, and then there came a strange half-hour when I couldn't find my way out of the wood although I knew it was small and on a hill and that going either up or down the slope in an approximately straight line would bring me to the edge. Shards of sunlight came through the trees. I tried to keep them on my left and head up hill, towards where I'd last heard Molly, but I couldn't hear her any more and the sun had got round to my right and I was getting so thirsty it was hard to think about anything but water, which I didn't have but the others did and anyway I couldn't be more than fifteen minutes from the hut and the stream and Mum who would have something I could eat. A bird sang insistently behind me, a shrill phrase repetitive as a telephone's bell. The tunic rasped my damp skin, clung to the still tender places on my back, and there were crumbs of earth and bark in the folds of my toes. Water. I needed water. The bird called again and I felt the sound shrill through my skull, reverberate in the gathering headache. I came to a thicket and turned to go down hill instead, switched the bag of nuts from one sore shoulder to the other. Of course I came out into the field, probably really quite fast; it was an acre of English woodland, not the Black Forest. After two fields I came to the stream and stopped to scoop water into my mouth and over my face. Never drink from the stream in sheep country, but the water was running fast enough and I was past caring.

Mum was sitting down again. Your dad came back, she said, he said to tell you you'll be needed tonight. I need a drink of water, I said. Is there anything I can eat? Not much, she said, I've not cooked. He said to tell you. What about the plums, I said, could I have some of those, you cooked them, right? They're very sour, she said, I don't know what folk did with them before they had sugar, you'd need a gill of honey and then some. I don't think I mind, I said, I'll eat them sour, but she was right, even for a hungry teenager a couple were enough. Acid yellow shrivelled plums and tepid water washed in my stomach. I thought about making bannocks, since Mum didn't seem to be about to do anything, since other people would be back and wanting to eat too, but I couldn't face being near the fire – Mum, I said, you've let the fire out. Well, she said, it's that hot, who's wanting one any road? Dad, I said, what do you think he'll say, what were you thinking, you know how he goes on about the fire and the hearth and all that, let's get it lit again quick, did he say when he'd be back. She sat down again. The fire were out when he came, she said, he's already seen it. You're too late, love, might as well sit down a minute.

I didn't ask her. I didn't want to know. If he had any sense, the bruises would come up in places where the rest of us didn't have to see them.

I thought I'd rest a while, keep her company, but there was no respite from the sun. Heat seemed to be reflecting off the land itself. I took a piece of cloth from the hut, left Mum folded where she was and went to dip my hair, my whole head, in the stream, kneeling fully clothed on the bank. As the water ran down my face, trickled warm between my breasts and down my back, I squatted on the bank to soak the linen cloth in fresh water for Mum. The bog myrtle grew there still cool and dark-leaved, so I picked a sprig for Mum and then had another idea and stripped a handful of new shoots, no more than two from each bush so the plants could recover quickly. I rubbed a leaf between my fingers and sniffed the balm, like lime and warm spices. When I was little I used to go to the bathroom and smell Mum's talc after I'd been smacked; I suppose I thought the scent might comfort her now. My wet hair was already warm on my neck as I walked back to the hut, the tunic damp and scratchy. Here, Mum, help you cool down a bit, I said. She didn't move. You'll maybe want to go into the hut and try a bit of a sponge bath, I said, feel a bit fresher, and look, I've bog myrtle for you, and when I helped her up she took it and went in. I squatted at the fireside, put down the bunch of myrtle for Molly, picked up a handful of warm ashes and watched it sift through my fingers. I remembered the ashes on the moor tops, the indecipherable fragments of bone. They did things with ashes, the Iron-Age Britons, made lime or potash or something. Or maybe that was later. The round stones ringing the fire were still warm. I sat down and used my new basket-weaving skills to make a crown of myrtle for Molly. I imagined its grey-green in her hair, the scent of it on her face.

Mum came out and sat down again. There were four fingermarks on her upper arm. It were my fault, she said, I knew how much he cares about the fire an' all. It's too hot, anyroad, I said, no-one's wanting fire.

We heard laughter and loud voices coming through the trees. I looked at my silly plaited crown and put it behind me. What had I been thinking, Molly wasn't six. Oh, Mum said, they've only gone and been to the bloody pub, that was all we needed, can you imagine. Maybe they're just happy, I said, high-spirited, but she shook her head and when they arrived I could see that she was right. We've not even got much they can eat to soak it up, she said, them plums aren't going to be any good, but Pete was carrying a bag of sliced white bread in each hand and Molly cradled a plastic bottle of lemonade. Here you go, Mrs Hampton, Pete said, it's no day to be slaving over a hot stove. Or campfire. Well, she said, what'll the Professor say to that, put it away, do. He'd probably want some himself, said Dan, anyway, I do. Look, we got some ham too. He pulled a transparent packet of flaccid pink slices out of his pocket.

Mum and I sat against the hut and watched them pass around the woolly bread and wet ham. I fiddled with the wreath at my side. Have some, Silvie, said Pete, you must be starving. Molly handed me the lemonade, too heavy for one hand. Here, it's for you, it was cold, I got them to put it in the chiller thing for wine, but it's probably warmed up now. I glanced up the hill, cocked an ear to the wood for Dad's footfall, and millimetre by millimetre unscrewed the hissing lid, hearing the pressure fall, feeling the slow release under my fingers. Beside me, Mum leant against the wall and let her eyes fix on nothing. Opposite, in the shade of the oak tree, knees apart like those of a child who doesn't know anyone cares about her knickers, Molly peeled a square slice of ham and lowered it onto her square of white bread, aligning the corners. Her lips and tongue reached as she took a large bite that left toothmarks in the flesh. She sucked salt from her index finger and then pushed a wisp of honey hair behind her ear. I looked up, saw Pete watching me watch her and blushed, felt the sudden heat in my face like pee in pants.

We heard the voices of Dad and the Prof an hour or so later. The others had gone off to cool down in the stream, the odd pulse of talk and laughter drifting back through the trees. Molly would be naked, I knew, or at best down to bright lace underwear and I couldn't still a beat of fear for her if Dad saw, although I knew he couldn't and wouldn't do anything worse than radiating rage and disgust. I had relit the fire and was feeding it and watching the new flames, ghostly in sunlight. Mum sat up as if her puppet-master had yanked her strings, and then lumbered to her feet. I haven't got the dinner on, she said, help me, Silvie. Well, I said, they didn't eat by the clock, did they, but I set the bag of hazelnuts conspicuously beside the log where Dad usually sat, and poured water into the cauldron so we could cook something. Whatever there was. How do you eat dried fish, I asked. In winter, said Mum, it spoilt in the sun, did you not notice, the smell was so bad I buried it, days since. So what is there now, I said. She shrugged. Hazelnuts. Mushrooms. A heel of white bread. Molly's laughter rang from the stream.

But they weren't angry. They drank a lot of water and opened and ate the nuts intently, chewing one while stripping the green shell from the next. Mum stood watching. Steam began to rise from the water which there was now no reason to heat.

Right, said the Prof, Silvie, can we have a word with

you, about the plan for tonight? It's something special. Come for a little stroll. I glanced at Mum, who didn't raise her eyes, and went.

They wanted to kill me at sunset. To march me up onto the moor to the beat of the drums and the bass chanting, to tie my hands and my feet, to put a rope around my neck that could be tightened and loosened for as long as blades and rocks could hold me wavering between life and death. Of course we won't actually hurt you, the Prof said, I hope you know that, Silvie. It's just the ritual we want to try, the way it must have looked and sounded, the drums on the moor and the winding of the ropes. I could feel my breathing tight, heat spreading from my chest into my arms. But we don't know, do we, I said, what it was like, you said there's no evidence, we know how they died but not why. That's why we should do this, he said, that's what we might learn. I promise you'll come to no harm. She knows that, said Dad, she's not daft. Are you, Silvie? Why does it have to be me, I said, although I knew the answer. Because I was the person you can hurt. Because I was the scapegoat, the sacrifice, the thing Dad wanted to keep. Well, said the Prof, they were mostly women, women and girls, and I can't ask Molly, she's a student and frankly her marks aren't great and I don't want her saying she was pressured into anything she didn't want to do, it could put me in a very difficult position. Your dad said you'd do it. Aye, and she will, said Dad, there's no call for all this fuss Silvie, it's just a bit of play-acting for the Professor's work. It sounds a bit weird, I said, I'm not sure, the ropes. He told you, said Dad, no-one's going to hurt you, we'll all be there, of course you'll do it. Now you go help your mum get a proper meal for everyone, it's going to be a long night.

The others were back from the stream, sitting damp and clean under a tree well away from the fire. Molly had a bowl of dough beside her and was shaping uneven flatbreads onto a platter where they would stick to it and each other. Mum was cutting up mushrooms with a flint knife. I went and sat by Molly and pulled off a handful of dough. So what was that about, she said, more bone-worship? I shook my head, found crying rising into my mouth and nose. Jesus, Silvie, what is it? I bit my lip, swallowed, bowed my head so the others wouldn't see. Not that they wouldn't see me tied up later, paraded in front of them. What, tell me! I squashed the ball of dough between my hands, tried to pat it out. It was too sticky, needed more meal. Molly put down her lump, stood up, rubbed her hands together. Come on, she said, come and talk. Mum needs these, I said, Dad said. Yes, well, she said, I say. Come on. Tell me what they said.

Dad had gone off to the wood, the Professor to write up his day. I finished forming the bread, picked up the wilted wreath from where I'd dropped it by the hut and walked behind Molly towards her tent. Maybe I could give it to her, after all. Moll's tent was like being inside a blue lampshade. She had an air mattress in there, a striped cotton sleeping-bag liner curled up like a discarded snakeskin, a sponge-bag unzipped and spilling bottles of nail-varnish and deodorant and face creams, a hairbrush webbed with pale hairs and a fruit salad of bobbles wound around its handle, crumpled crisp-packets and sweet wrappers in a pile in the corner, a couple of battered paperback novels. The tent had the apple smell of Molly. We sat in the entrance, as if the tent fabric meant we wouldn't be heard. Molly, I said, look, I made something for you, it's silly but I thought you might like it, the smell, here. I blushed again. Hey, she said, you made me a crown, thanks Silvie. She took it and put it on her barley-coloured hair and my hand reached out to stroke. No. I took the hand back. It's bog myrtle, I said, I like the smell, you can rub it between your fingers, I expect they used it, then, maybe even in the bedding, it smells clean. Like you, I thought, it smells like you, but I didn't say so. I like it, she said, I'm the midsummer queen, thank you. Now what's this about, Sil, tell me. So I told her, more or less.

They're insane, she said, no way, they've completely lost the plot. You're not doing that, no way. And I'm sorry, Silvie. I'm sorry they thought they could ask you. She put her arm round me. I didn't cry. I rested my head on her shoulder, breathed her in. Stay with me, OK, she said, just stay near me and I won't let them do anything, I promise. She stroked my hair. Don't, I said, it's filthy, I probably smell. You don't smell, she said, anyway everyone smells a bit in this heat. You told them you won't do it, right? I shook my head. I can't, I said, Dad would be furious, you have to see that, I can't. Silvie, she said, you can't let them tie you up and pretend to kill you either, you do know that, you either have to say no or you'll have to go through with it, and you're not doing that so you have to tell them. Just say you changed your mind. Say you talked to me and I told you not to, they won't do anything to me. I can't, I said, I'm sorry Molly, I'm sorry but I can't. Shaking came from deep inside. I can't. Dad— Your dad's not God, she said, he can't do anything he likes to you. I know, I said, he's not, it's OK, I'll be all right, they did ask. Oh Silvie, she said. Oh Sulevia, goddess of the groves.

Mum had rescued the flatbreads and cooked the mushrooms, but I couldn't eat. Filled yourself up with bubbles, Mum murmured, you'll be hungry again before bed. The boys, presumably sobered by the stream and the bread, finished everything, and after some goading from Molly went to wash the plates. The sun came down into the trees. I'll come with you to tell them, said Molly, or you go rest in my tent and I'll say you changed your mind, you can't do this, it's ridiculous and stupid and wrong in every way. I shook my head. It was too late. They're not going to hurt me, I said, I know that, I just wish – I couldn't even say it. I wish I didn't have to be tied up in front of everyone. I wish my father didn't want to put a rope around my neck. It doesn't matter, I said, it will all be over by morning. Maybe it will be interesting after all. No, she said. No, you can't do this, they're insane.

Mum was putting the turfs on the fire and I went to help her. Thanks, she said, is summat up, seems Molly's in a bit of a taking? I knelt up. There was no point, I knew, there was nothing Mum could do, no point in telling her. I remembered her arm, the marks you get if you resist when someone's trying to hit you, if you make him have to hold you down. Better just to take what's coming to you anyway. Not that I know of, I said, you know she gets a mood on when she thinks the lads aren't pulling their weight.

And come the moment, Molly wasn't there. The Prof appeared with a camera strung around his neck – we might want to publish on this later, he said, I don't think anyone's done it before – and Dad laid a skein of rough rope around mine. We made it, he said proudly, it's what we were doing yesterday, turns out it's not hard to reach a fair breaking strain. It was heavy on my collarbones, itchy on my neck. He tied it behind me, somewhere between my shoulder blades, and caught some of my greasy hair in the knot. Not the hangman's knot, said the Prof, it wasn't meant to break the neck, remember? A slow dying, strangulation, in the end. We won't tie her hands yet, the Prof said, don't want you falling over on the way, do we Silvie?

I couldn't look up. With a rope lying around my neck, I couldn't meet his eyes. He took a picture of me. As I looked away I caught Pete's grin.

Silvie, said Dan, Silvie, are you really OK with this, are you sure about it? Of course she is, said Dad, she knows we won't hurt her, she's not stupid.

Silvie, said Dan.

I nodded. Yeah, it's OK.

You lead her, Bill, said the Professor, after all I suppose she's your sacrifice.

The shadows were long in the grass, the whole moorland low and still in slanting yellow light. In the east the trees stood dark against the sky and all the colours were fading. A late flight of birds winged the air, homeward bound.

Dad walked in front of me, so that the rope pulled and loosened on the back of my neck and was always before my eyes. I could feel my hair catching and tangling around it but when I tried to gather my hair in my hand I lost my balance and stumbled. That's what'll happen if you don't watch where you're going, said Dad. Silvie, said Dan, you all right? Yeah, I said, fine.

When I could stay in step with Dad, the rope's loop swung between us, but mostly I couldn't and it tautened and fell, its shadow scribbling over the heather along the path. When we got to the bog, I thought, they – Dad, probably – would tie my hands behind my back, and the rope would be scratchy. The bog people didn't struggle, went with dignity. Don't fight, don't panic. I remembered then Dad saying the blindfolds and gags were to protect the killers from the dying, but I didn't know any curses and I didn't think they, Dad and the Prof, would be scared of what was behind my eyes.

Behind me, Pete and Dan began to beat their drums, a rhythm slower than my heart but too fast for my feet.

We came to the bog. The sun was still above the rocks, there was still time. Strip her, said the Prof. Dad turned me to face the darkening water while the others watched him tie my wrists behind me. I held them back-to-back for him and immediately regretted it; my fingers would have liked the comfort of each other's grasp. The boys were drumming still, the beat spreading across the dim moor, pulsing through marsh and reed, under the small shelter of the heather towards the mound on the horizon. There, said Dad. It was too tight, but perhaps any rope around your wrists is too tight. I found myself standing straighter, shoulders back. A wind came licking over the cotton grass, lifted my hair. And her legs, said Dad. Not yet, said the Prof, that comes later. Unless she tries to fight. Turn her to face us.

The drums beat. The chanting began. I didn't join in this time but stood before them, bound and yet now no longer afraid or ashamed. Here I am then. So kill me.

They put a fresh flint blade to my hairline. There on her face for the shame of it maybe, I remembered Dad saying. Dad took his hunting knife to my arm, looked me in the face as he pressed down. Here and here, just done for the pain like. I held his gaze. The moon rose, full. They came at me with sticks raised and I lost my balance and fell on the water's edge, was set on my feet again for more. For as long as I could, I watched the infinitesimal progress of the moon along the darkening sky, listened to the calls of the last birds crossing the cool of the evening. There was pain. They had a pile of stones, ready.

Molly brought two policemen as well as Trudi. I was still standing with the bog at my back which meant that I saw the torches coming up the moor and said nothing, gave no warning. Which meant that it was my fault when they arrested Dad.

TRUDI AND MOLLY untied the ropes. They had brought a blanket to wrap around me, although I was not cold, and they led me away, the light of Trudi's torch scrolling the path ahead as the sun, at last, left us to the dark and the moon. It's over, Silvie, said Molly, we're looking after you now. Angry male voices came on the rising wind.

A police car and a small red car sat by the gate where the moorland track came down to the lane. Here, said Trudi, Molly, would you sit in the back with Silvie? If you're all right with it, Silvie, we'll just pop you round to the doctor now, he's waiting to check you over, and then I'm taking you back to my house for the night. You'll have to share with Molly but you'll be safe and dry. It's dry outside, I thought, but I said what about Mum, and my dad, he won't like it. And I don't need a doctor, really, I'm fine. Someone will tell your mum, said Trudi, and as for your dad – well, he should just be glad to know that you're being cared for. Don't worry about him. The doctor's no bother, he's already been called, might as well have him look at you. It might help later, Silvie.

Molly and I hadn't fastened our seat belts and we bumped and leaned together as Trudi flung her car around corners and over hills. No, I said, I don't want to, I don't need anyone looking at me. Are you quite sure about that, Silvie, said Trudi. Are you sure there's nothing you might wish we'd recorded, later? Someone cut you, didn't they, and I saw a stick in that boy's hand. Pete, I said, that was Pete, Dan left, quite early. Before the – the knife. Yeah, I'm sure. The car swung again, lurched. Molly put her arm around me. You're OK now, she said. I went to the phone box and called my mum and she said call the police and find Trudi. What will the police do, I said, to my dad? Trudi glanced back in the dark. Whatever they think best, she said, Molly did the right thing and it's out of our hands now. Branches and green leaves stood out spotlit as we rounded a corner. We slowed, turned, bumped along uneven ground. The handbrake squawked as Trudi pulled it up. She turned off the engine but left the lights on as she said Silvie, people will be asking you this again in the next few days but I have to ask you one more time, how much did they hurt you, apart from those cuts did anyone touch you in ways you didn't like or didn't want? No, I said, no, there was nothing, they did ask me and I could have said no. Are you quite sure about that, she said, because you know in some cases we might want to take some samples, to do an examination, before you get in the shower? We can go over to the surgery right now, it won't take long, I could do the exam myself if you prefer. No, I said, no, there was nothing like that. He's my dad. I don't need to see a doctor. Yes, Trudi said, if you're certain, if you're quite sure.

In her untidy sitting room, Trudi took out her midwife's bag and cleaned the cuts on my arm with something that stung. Close your eyes, she said, the one here doesn't look too bad. She handed me a white cotton dressing like a sanitary pad. Apply pressure, she said, the bleeding's pretty much stopped anyway, I'll dress those properly when you've had a shower, don't think we need stitches. They hurt again, blood trickled, when I took a shower in Trudi's pink bathroom, raised my stiff arms to wash my hair in some stuff with a grown-up smell. I craned to see in the mirror the marks on my back fading, and the soft cream towel barely hurt my legs although my arm left smears of blood on it. There were sore patches now on my wrists and maybe some bruises coming but Trudi was right, the cut on my face was barely there at all, a red biro line already taut. I wrapped the towel around me when she knocked on the door and came in with a gust of cold air and a clean nightie and the dressing for my arm. I saw her glance at my shoulders but she said nothing. Here we go then, let's get those cuts covered, shall we.

Trudi had made up a bed on the floor for Molly, beside the single bed which she said was for me, and when I came out of the bathroom in the nightie, Moll sat up. Oh Silvie, she said, the marks are still there, you poor love, and she knelt and touched my thighs with her cool fingers. I looked down at her golden hair, her breasts free under a borrowed T-shirt, and she stood up and held me, her arms gentle against my back. I laid my face against her hair and thought that as I breathed in I could still somehow catch inside me the scent of her bog myrtle crown. Stay with me, I said, please, just tonight. She moved away and pulled back the worn brown duvet cover for me. Lie down, she said, I'll be on the outside, you'll know I'm between you and everything else, and then she curled around me, her bare legs cradling mine, her fingers at rest on my belly, her breathing warm on my shoulder, and I lay watching the full moon and then the dawn through the ivy-framed window of Trudi's cottage the rest of that short summer night.

Acknowledgements

This book began in two places: the first when I participated in a residency in Northumberland to celebrate the tenth anniversary of the Hexham Literary Festival. I thank Susie Troup for inviting me and looking after me there; Claire and Hilary of Cogito Books in Hexham for their kindness to a wandering writer; Wendy Breach at Bridge House for providing the perfect base. Most of all I thank Andy Bates, who taught me everything I know about leather, replicas and re-enactment, and introduced me to the bog people. All errors of fact or probability are my own, but most of the truths are ones he told me.

My second inspiration was the 'Scotland's People' exhibition in the National Museum of Scotland, where

I went to spend time with the possessions and bodies of Iron and Bronze Age residents of the borderlands. I am grateful to Dr Fraser Hunter, Principal Curator of Iron Age and Roman Collections, who took some trouble to find and send me Pat McGuire's haunting notes for the 'Dead and Sometimes Buried' exhibition when I suddenly decided I needed them.

I thank my colleagues in the Warwick Writing Programme and in the English Department at Warwick: Will Eaves, Maureen Freely, AL Kennedy, Tim Leach, Tina Lupton, David Morley and Chantal Wright.

Thank you, as always, to Sinéad Mooney for early reading; to Kathy MacDonald for archaeological conversations; to Anna Webber at United Agents for sage counsel and afternoon tea as well as excellent representation; to everyone at Granta Books, especially the brilliant Lamorna Elmer, and Max Porter, my editor and my friend.